MW00648834

# Where the

# Rainbow

# Ends

Diego and Izzy
Summer Lake Silver Book Four

By SJ McCoy

A Sweet n Steamy Romance

Published by Xenion, Inc

Copyright © 2020 SJ McCoy

WHERE THE RAINBOW ENDS Copyright © SJ McCoy 2020

Published by Xenion, Inc.
First paperback edition 2020
www.sjmccoy.com

This book is a work of fiction. Names, characters, places, and events
are figments of the author's imagination, fictitious, or are used
fictitiously. Any resemblance to actual events, locales or persons
living or dead is coincidental.

Cover Design by Dana Lamothe of Designs by Dana
Cover Model: Christopher Clark
Cover Photography by Golden Czermak of Furious Fotog

Editor: Mitzi Pummer Carroll
Proofreaders: Aileen Blomberg, Traci Atkinson.

ISBN: 978-1-946220-69-1

# Dedication

*For Chris.*

*I'm so honoured to have your photo grace the cover of Diego and Izzy's story, and thrilled that this gets to be your first published book.*

*I have no doubt that this will be the first of many covers for you, and before long you'll have a whole bookcase full of them.*

*I want to thank you for adding a touch of who you are to Diego's character. He's a good guy — not nearly the person Izzy initially judged him to be. And with just a few words you made him a better man.*

*Here's wishing you much success in your career.*

*And much love and happiness in your life.*

*Love*

*SJ*

*oxo*

# Chapter One

Diego looked around the crowded bar. It was much busier than usual here in the Boathouse tonight. It was a younger crowd than usual, too. He wasn't above admiring the younger women, even flirting with them, but that was as far as he would take it. He shuddered. Most of the women here tonight looked to be the same age as his son, Zack—perhaps younger. Some men were attracted to women half their age, but Diego wasn't one of them.

His friend, Ted, raised an eyebrow at him. "I'm not sure how long I'm going to stay tonight. I think it's going to be too busy and too loud for my taste."

Diego smiled at him. "I don't like to admit it, but I think I'll be ready to leave whenever you are. Zack and Maria aren't coming, so I don't think we need to sit here propping up the bar all night—" He stopped when someone elbowed him. He turned to see what was going on.

The woman gave him an apologetic smile. "I'm sorry."

He smiled. "That's okay. No problem." He was pleased to see someone his own age here—and an attractive someone at that. As he started to turn back to Ted, he caught sight of her companion. Another woman his own age, but if the first one was attractive, this one was gorgeous! He forced himself to turn back to Ted.

He grinned at his friend and jerked his head, indicating that he should take a look for himself.

Ted couldn't get a good look around Diego, so he turned to check them out in the mirror behind the bar. His expression changed when he saw them, and Diego could only hope that he preferred the one who'd elbowed him. He smirked and mouthed, *wow!*

To his surprise, Ted shook his head rapidly.

"What?"

Ted looked stunned. "That's *her*."

"Her who? Oh!" Diego grinned. "Your friend from the gym? Your beautiful mess?"

Ted nodded.

"So, what are you waiting for?" Diego began to turn around, but Ted caught his arm.

"Give me a minute."

"If you say so."

They both stayed quiet, and Diego felt bad eavesdropping on their conversation. It seemed that the one who'd elbowed him had her ex-husband here tonight. And the gorgeous blonde was being supportive. He liked her for that. In his experience, women were sometimes less than supportive of each other. He could only guess that was due to their own insecurities. He wanted to believe that the blonde didn't have any of those.

He, too, was now watching the pair in the mirror behind the bar.

When the song ended, the blonde waggled her eyebrows. "Come on, Audrey, you can't tell me you'd turn the drummer down if he asked you? He's hot!"

Diego pursed his lips. If he had to compete with another man for the blonde's attention, he'd rather it wasn't the drummer—who just happened to be Ted's son.

He watched her friend, wondering whether she also would be interested in a much younger man.

"You know me, Izzy," said the friend.

Izzy? It wasn't a name he'd heard before; he wondered what it was short for.

"That guy is your type," the friend continued. "I, on the other hand, wish I could meet his father."

Well, that was good news for Ted, at least! Diego spun around to look at him with a big grin on his face. "Sorry, mi amigo, but I must." He turned back toward the women, put his hand on the friend's shoulder, and said, "Wish granted."

She looked confused, and Diego realized that she must think he meant he was Eddie's father. He leaned back so that she could see Ted sitting beside him.

There was no mistaking the moment that they shared. Diego had never seen Ted look so smitten.

Ted got down from his seat and went to shake the woman's hand. "It's a pleasure to see you again. I'm Ted." He jerked his head toward the stage. "And that's my son, Eddie."

She cleared her throat. "It's nice to see you again."

It seemed that she was as smitten as Ted. Diego saw Izzy kick her foot, startling her back to her senses. "I'm Audrey, and this is Izzy."

Finally, the blonde looked at Diego, and his heart began to race. She grinned and leaned forward to shake first his hand and then Ted's. "How do you two know each other?" she asked.

"We met briefly this morning," said Ted.

"Oh! You're the guy from the gym!"

Diego grinned. Ted had mentioned earlier that he'd had a moment with a woman in the gym this morning. And it seemed that fortune had smiled on them so that their paths now crossed again. He could only hope that Lady Luck was feeling as benevolent toward him.

He held his hand out to shake with Izzy and nodded at Audrey. "I heard about this brief meeting, too." He gave Izzy a conspiratorial smile. "I'm Diego, by the way. Since Ted seems to have forgotten to introduce me. Can we buy you a drink, ladies?"

Izzy waved a bottle of champagne. "We're fine for drinks, thanks. But we'd love for you to join us."

"Another bottle, then." Diego grinned. He was thrilled at the invitation. "And tell us what you're celebrating, so we can join in?"

"It's my—" began Audrey.

"Audrey here is beginning a new chapter," Izzy spoke over her.

Diego waved the bartender, Kenzie, over to order more champagne. They were drinking Veuve Clicquot, and he was happy to join them.

"What kind of chapter?" asked Ted.

Izzy answered the question for her. "Audrey's had a tough time for the last few years, and now she's coming into her own." She raised her glass and smiled at them. "She's ready to have some fun."

Diego held up a fresh bottle of champagne and two more glasses. "May I suggest that we move to a table? The band is about to take their break, and that will mean a rush at the bar." It wasn't purely self-interest that made him want to move away from the bar. Of course, he was hoping to get to know Izzy better, but Ted and Audrey had hardly taken their eyes off each other yet.

Izzy slid down from her stool with a grin. "I was just thinking the same thing. There's a booth open over there, see?"

Ted and Audrey hung back while he and Izzy made their way to the booth. Diego hesitated for a moment, then decided that sitting opposite her would be best.

She smiled at him. "Are you guys locals?"

"No. We live in Laguna Beach. You?"

"No. We're just here for the weekend. We live in Ventura."

Diego smiled. That was closer to home than here. He caught himself mid-thought. What did it even matter where she lived? Sure, she was an attractive woman, but she was interested in Ted's son. What made him think that she might have any interest in him? He smiled to himself. There was only one way to find out.

At that moment, Ted and Audrey came to sit with them. Ted slid into the seat beside him, and Diego slid a glass of champagne in front of him. Attractive as Izzy was, Ted was his main priority tonight. He hadn't shown any interest in a woman for a long time—and he was the kind of man who should be with someone. He had a big heart and a kind soul. They'd been friends for over twenty-five years, and Diego would love to see him find a woman and the kind of happiness he deserved.

Ted raised his glass to Audrey. "To new beginnings."

"New beginnings," Audrey echoed.

Diego smiled as he raised his glass. He'd put money on the fact that he was witnessing a new beginning between the two of them.

"So," Izzy grinned around at them, "we know that Eddie is your son, and Diego tells me that you guys live in Laguna Beach. What else do we need to know about you?"

Diego got the impression that she was as protective of her friend as he was of his.

"What do you want to know?" asked Ted.

"Everything." She looked more serious as she continued. "I suppose the first important thing to get out of the way is, where's Eddie's mom?"

Diego caught Ted's eye. He knew the score. Eddie's mom had cheated on Ted, and they'd divorced less than amicably. She'd ensured that Ted hadn't been part of Eddie's life for the longest time.

"Where is she?" asked Ted. "I have no idea. I haven't seen or heard from her in …" He had to think about it. "almost twenty-five years."

Izzy looked thrilled to hear it. Although apparently, she hadn't picked up on how uncomfortable the question had made Ted.

"What about you, Audrey?" Diego didn't see why Ted should be the only one to have to put it all out there.

Ted turned to glare at him. Perhaps he shouldn't have put her on the spot like that.

"I've been divorced for almost three years now. Unfortunately, I can't say I haven't seen him in that time. In fact, he's here this evening. This is our children's birthday party."

"And what about you, Diego?" Ted glared at him.

Diego shrugged. He smiled at Audrey. "My son lives here, also. His name is Zack. His mother left us when he was six."

"I'm sorry." Audrey's expression said a lot about her.

"And before anyone asks me to share my tale of woe," said Izzy. "I have no children. I couldn't, and I've been divorced for eight years from a man who swore to me that it didn't matter. He's remarried with a six-year-old daughter." Diego's heart hurt for her. She smiled as she said it, but he could see pain in her eyes.

"Well." Audrey looked around the table. "Now that we've got that out of the way ..." She smiled. "Perhaps we can bring it back to regular chitchat. Are you two here for the weekend? Where's home?"

"Home is Laguna Beach. And I'm here for the week." Ted smiled. "My grandson asked me to stay."

Diego cocked his head to one side. "Did I know this?"

Ted laughed. "I thought I told you, but perhaps I forgot."

Diego shrugged and looked at Izzy. "I'm going home to Laguna tomorrow. You?"

She grinned. "I have to go home tomorrow, too." She turned to Audrey. "But this one is staying until next weekend, while I go back and run the office."

Audrey laughed. "Don't go for the sympathy vote. You're the one who insisted I take some time off. I can come back with you if you like."

Izzy shook her head rapidly. "No way!"

Diego sensed that the dynamic between the two of them was similar to the one he and Ted shared. It made him smile. What made him smile even more was the fact that she was leaving tomorrow. Right now, she seemed more interested in helping Ted and Audrey along, but if she showed an interest in him, then he saw no reason he shouldn't give her a ride home tomorrow. Ventura might be a couple hundred miles from Laguna, but in the jet, that was hardly any time at all.

~ ~ ~

"What are your plans while you're here?" Ted asked Audrey.

She smiled at him. "To rest and relax."

"To have some fun," added Izzy. She couldn't believe that Audrey was so taken with Ted. She hadn't shown any interest in guys since her divorce. Izzy caught Ted's gaze and gave him the hint of a nod.

"Perhaps you can both have some fun," said Diego.

Izzy wanted to laugh at the expressions on Audrey and Ted's faces. She and Diego were both being a little over the top, and she knew it.

"Would you excuse me for a moment?" Audrey asked. "The kids are coming over."

When Izzy followed her gaze, she saw Audrey's kids, Ally and Brayden, talking to the drummer—Ted's son.

She gave Diego a rueful smile when the other two went to talk to their kids. "Is he as good a guy as he seems to be?"

A wave of heat rushed through her when he turned his smile on her. She'd been trying to ignore it ever since the moment she laid eyes on him, but he was one fine man! She drew in an unsteady breath. The trouble was, he was all man. She could just tell that he was one of those big macho guys.

"He's even better. He's a kind soul and a good man."

He held her gaze for a long and moment, and she found it hard to drag her eyes away. She hadn't expected him to talk like that. Guys like him didn't have souls as far as she was concerned, they certainly didn't recognize kindness in others' souls.

"And Audrey?" he asked.

She nodded. "His only concern with her should be not to hurt her. She's not someone who does this kind of thing."

She watched a little smirk play on his lips and couldn't help noticing how full they were and wondering what it would be like to kiss them. She pulled herself together.

"You're the wiser one, looking out for her?"

She nodded.

He raised one eyebrow, and his voice resonated through her, turning her on more than she would admit even to herself. "Wiser, because you *do* do this sort of thing?"

She held his gaze for a long moment.

"Would you want to do *this* sort of thing?" He let his gaze travel over her, and her body reacted as though it were his fingers touching her.

She sucked in a deep breath to steady herself and shook her head slowly.

His smile faded a little. "No?"

"I think our purpose tonight is to look out for our friends, don't you?"

He nodded.

She'd only intended to buy herself a little time. If she told him that yes, she would love to do that sort of thing with him … she shuddered. He was the kind of guy she stayed clear of. Big, macho, full-on personality.

It seemed he'd taken her rejection as complete. He turned to watch Audrey and Ted talking to their children.

"That's Ted's son, talking with them."

She nodded.

"Ah, of course, you knew this. He's the drummer in the band."

She swung her head to look at him, but he continued to watch Audrey and Ted. Had he heard what she'd said about Eddie earlier? She felt like he must have. He'd taken her hesitation toward his own advances to mean rejection and then immediately focused on Eddie—the guy she'd made no secret about finding attractive.

She almost wanted to rescue the moment. She felt drawn to Diego in a way that she hadn't felt with a guy in years. He might be big and macho and over-the-top, but he was also sexy-as-sin; it'd be a shame to pass up on that. But no. She had a deal with herself these days. She only got involved—and involved was far too strong a term for the kind of liaisons she had—with younger guys these days. There were fewer chances of complications that way.

She looked at him again, but he was smiling as he watched Audrey and Ted. She turned to see why. Audrey's ex, Richard, was shaking hands with Ted, and Izzy liked Ted that little bit more when she saw the look of distaste on his face. Diego claimed that he was a man of good character—she could see for herself that he was, at least, a good judge of character.

When they came and sat back down, Izzy grinned at Audrey. "I see you had the chance to talk with Richard?"

She nodded.

Diego grinned at Ted. "Judging by the way he was so eager to meet you, I'd guess that he knew who you are?"

Ted smiled back at him. "He did."

Audrey turned to look at him. "It seems he's more in the know than I am."

"He's probably heard mention of me in business circles."

Diego chuckled. "My friend is too modest. I, on the other hand, am not. We're bankers. Rawlins-Águila is a well-known and respected private bank."

Izzy raised her eyebrows. "So, Ted Rawlins and Diego Águila?"

"That's right."

"And what about you, ladies?" asked Ted. "What do you do?"

"Advertising," said Audrey.

"Do you work for anyone we might know?" asked Diego.

Izzy laughed. It was typical that he would assume they worked for someone else. "We both work for someone you know: Audrey."

"You have your own agency?" asked Ted. "Where are you based?"

"The office is in Ventura. We're just a small team."

Izzy rolled her eyes and looked at Diego. "My friend is as bad as yours for being overly modest. She went out on her own after her divorce from *him*. You know what the name Richard usually gets shortened to, don't you? Well, in his case, there couldn't be a more appropriate nickname."

"Izzy!" Audrey made a face at her.

Diego looked puzzled for a moment, then laughed when he figured out what Izzy meant. That surprised her. She'd have expected him to be quicker than that, but perhaps it was a language thing. His accent wasn't too strong—in fact, it was perfectly sexy—but it was enough to say that English wasn't his first language.

"Anyway," she continued forcing herself to focus on the conversation instead of thinking about his deep sexy voice. "The two of them were in business together. Audrey did all the work. But the advertising world is still like an old boys' club. So, when they separated, most of the business stayed with Richard. He's pretty much run the agency into the ground now, from what I hear."

"That's not true," said Audrey.

Izzy held up a hand. "Okay. Sorry. I'll stop." She smiled at Ted and Diego. "The short version of the story is that Audrey went out on her own after the divorce and now runs a digital advertising agency that has won numerous awards in the last couple of years."

Ted caught Audrey's eye. "What kind of clients do you work with?"

Diego chuckled. "I think he's wondering whether you work with banks."

Izzy glanced at him. It was a stupid thought, but she hoped that it might work out that way. If Audrey wanted to work with Ted, that would mean that she'd get to see Diego again. Though why she would want to …

Audrey smiled. "We work with anyone who's looking to increase their reach online. But I'm here to take a break from work. So, if you don't mind, can we move the conversation along?"

"Why don't we move it onto the dance floor?" suggested Diego.

Izzy was on her feet in a moment. It was only because she wanted to get away from the conversation. Dancing would be a good distraction from sitting there staring across the table into Diego's big gorgeous eyes!

The dance floor was crowded, but Diego took hold of her hand and went ahead of her, clearing a path for them. For a moment, she let herself relax and enjoy the feeling. He was a big guy, and there was something commanding about him, too. People gave way to him, and the thought crossed her mind of how it would feel if she gave way to him. Shivers chased each other down her spine as she looked at his broad back. But no.

When he stopped and turned to look at her, Izzy let go of his hand and elbowed a space for herself. She was perfectly capable of making her own way in the world—she didn't need a man to do it for her.

She was relieved when Audrey and Ted made their way out onto the dance floor. She didn't want to be left out here with just Diego. He was a great dancer, which didn't surprise her. He was one of those guys who would be good at everything he did; she could just tell. Her concern was that if she wasn't careful, he'd be doing her before the night was out.

# Chapter Two

Diego's heart was racing in his chest when the cab pulled up outside the lodge. He had a sense of impending disappointment. The rest of the evening had gone well. Ted and Audrey were so into each other it was obvious. He had a feeling that it might be just as obvious how into Izzy he was, but she kept fending him off. He wasn't averse to laying on the charm to win a woman over, but her comment about Eddie kept plaguing him. She'd shot him down every time he'd made any kind of advance toward her, and he knew that he should just let it be. If the two of them were staying here the whole week like Ted and Audrey, then he'd no doubt make more of an effort, but she was leaving. So was he. That would have to be an end to it.

Izzy jumped out of the cab, and he quickly followed her. They were no doubt going to bid Ted and Audrey goodnight right here, but he couldn't stand the thought of Izzy scurrying away from him without so much as a proper goodbye. He smiled to himself ruefully while he waited for the others to get out of the cab; he had a feeling that she was going to be the one who got away. He at least wanted a peck before she went.

As the cab pulled away, they all stood at the bottom of the steps that led up to the lobby.

"A drink in the bar, then?" asked Ted.

Audrey nodded and looked at the others.

Izzy slipped her arm through Diego's, making his heart race. "I'm afraid I'm absolutely pooped," she said.

A ball of disappointment settled in his stomach. She wasn't eager to have a drink with him. She was giving their friends the chance to be alone. He faked a big yawn. His own chances might be disappearing before his eyes, but he was still happy for Ted. "I also am too tired."

Ted laughed. "Can you make it any more obvious, guys?"

Izzy laughed. "You're the one who isn't going along with it. We tried. You two go ahead. Have a drink; we'll see you tomorrow."

Diego took hold of Audrey's hand and kissed the back of it. "It was a pleasure to meet you." That was the truth. She was a good woman, he could tell. And if she could make Ted happy, then he would be happy for them.

"It was lovely to meet you, too."

Ted smiled at Izzy.

She waved a hand. "No need to say anything. I'll see you tomorrow."

Diego's heart leapt into his throat at that. If she expected to see Ted tomorrow, then there was no reason she wouldn't see him, too.

He looked down at her and tightened his arm so that she wouldn't pull hers away as they walked up the steps into the lodge.

Once they were inside, she glanced back over her shoulder.

"Are they coming?" he asked.

"No. I have a feeling they're going to go for a walk first."

Diego smiled. "Ted loves to walk on the beach."

She laughed. "They're perfect for each other. Audrey does, too."

She turned back and started walking toward the elevators. Diego decided he might as well give it a shot. He started steering her toward the bar.

She gave him a puzzled look.

"Since it's unlikely that they're going to come in and go to the bar, I think we should be safe, don't you?"

"Safe?"

He held her gaze for a long moment. He had to resist the urge to tell her that she was safe with him. Most women liked to hear that, liked to feel that way. With Izzy, he got the feeling that she wouldn't want to hear it. "Safe to have a nightcap at the bar."

She pursed her lips.

"I wouldn't normally come back early. I get the impression that you wouldn't either. We're trying to do a good deed for our friends. I think we at least deserve a drink as our reward." Why was he justifying it that way? He didn't understand himself. He didn't need an excuse to ask a beautiful woman if she wanted a nightcap with him. He didn't usually have any doubt that a beautiful woman would accept eagerly, either. But Izzy wasn't just a beautiful woman. She was a smart, independent woman. And for some reason, he got the impression that everything that most women found attractive about him turned her off somehow.

Still, he risked it. He let his gaze travel over her—and not only because he knew the effect it had on women, but also because she was so gorgeous. He'd been drinking her in with his eyes every chance he got all night. If this was going to be his last chance, he didn't want to lose it.

When he looked back into her eyes, he was surprised—and turned on—to see something that looked a lot like lust in them.

She nodded slowly. "You're right. We shouldn't miss out on a good time just because they're having one."

His heart began to race. Was she talking about the kind of good time he'd like to have with her?

She laughed as if she'd read his mind and started walking toward the bar. "Don't go getting any ideas, handsome. My idea of a good time right now is a good stiff—"

He couldn't help but laugh. "I can help with that!"

She rolled her eyes at him, even as she laughed. "No. We need to be straight about this. No, you can't help with that."

His heart sank. "No?"

She shook her head, but her eyes belied her words. She was attracted to him, he could tell. "You're not my type. I can see the appeal, but …"

He shrugged. He wasn't one to beg a woman. He was more used to them coming on strong to him. He felt that ball of disappointment in his stomach tighten. If her type was someone like Eddie—a younger guy—then there was nothing he could do about that.

He blew out an exaggerated sigh. "Very well. You break my heart. However, I am nothing but gracious in defeat." They reached the bar, and he steered her toward a booth in the back.

She raised an eyebrow at him. "You still want to sit back here?"

He chuckled. "I don't want people to see me crying into my drink."

"You're hardly going to do that. I thought you might prefer to sit at the bar so you can check out your options for when I go up to bed."

His head jerked up at that. He couldn't deny that he'd been known to move on to another woman in a bar if his first conversation fell flat.

She laughed. "You've done it. Don't try to deny it."

"I won't. Although, that's not my intention tonight." He raised an eyebrow at her and smirked. "You think I have accepted defeat? I haven't given up hope yet."

A smile played on her lips.

"That's funny?" he asked.

She shrugged. "You surprise me, I suppose. I thought my rejection might have been too big a hit to your ego." She looked around. "It seems to me that you have a few options in here that could help you salve it."

He smiled at her through pursed lips. "It seems to me that your rejection isn't as complete as you'd like me to believe." He was gratified to see her eyes widen at that. It gave him hope, and he had to test it. He leaned forward, dangerously close to her. Her eyes grew wider still, and he couldn't help but notice the way her breasts rose and fell as she breathed more deeply.

He reached past her and plucked a single flower from the vase on the table. There were only inches between them now, and he could honestly say that he could help her with that good stiff …

She took the flower from him with a smile and sat back. "Thank you. That's sweet of you."

He held her gaze for a long moment. He'd been right. Her rejection of him was far from complete. He knew that if he wanted to work hard for it, he could probably convince her to drop her defenses completely. He could charm his way into her bed tonight; he was fairly sure of it. What he wasn't sure of was whether he wanted to. She'd told him he wasn't her type. She hadn't told him, but he knew that she liked younger guys. Why would he put himself out there for that?

The waiter came, and they ordered their drinks. It gave Izzy enough time to compose herself. When Diego had leaned in close like that, it'd almost been game over! He'd invaded all her senses. He was a lot of man. He was maybe six-two. Broad shoulders. Big, strong arms. She shivered and twirled the flower he'd given her. Powerful. That was the word that came to mind. And it was a word that freaked her out. She peeked at him.

He was watching her with that damned little smirk playing on his lips. She bit the inside of her cheek at the thought that she'd like to kiss that smirk right off his face. What was she thinking? He was someone she would never get involved with—not even for a night. Despite the effect he had on her physically, she just couldn't handle it. She was nobody's second-in-command. And that's what guys like Diego wanted—at best. He needed to be the star of the show, and any woman would have to play a supporting role. She bit back a laugh—even in bed! That wasn't her thing.

He raised an eyebrow at her. "Something funny?"

She shrugged. "Just life."

"Tell me about yours? You live in Ventura. You work with Audrey. What else?"

"There's not much else to know. You heard my history when we were all coming clean back at the Boathouse." She frowned as a thought struck her. "What about you? You're a banker. You don't strike me as a banker."

His smile was just so damned sexy. There was something inviting about it—something dangerous, at least dangerous for her. Strangely enough, she got the feeling that it was only dangerous because she knew how to take care of herself. If she wanted or needed a man to take care of her, then it would most likely be more reassuring.

"I don't see myself as one either. It's kind of where Ted and I landed in life, if not where we set out to be."

She frowned. "What, you made so much money that you had to open your own bank?"

He chuckled. "Something like that."

"What else?" She was curious now to know about him. "Your son lives here?"

"That's right, he and his fiancée, Maria. I come up to visit as often as I can."

"And there's no Mrs. Águila?" It wouldn't surprise her if he said that yes there was.

He frowned. "I told you, she left us when Zack was six."

"She was the only one?"

He frowned again. She got the impression that he wasn't used to women questioning him. She bit back a smile. He was probably more used to them agreeing with him—loudly. Along the lines of *yes, Diego, yes!* She shifted in her seat at the thought of breathing those words herself.

"She was."

Izzy came back to her senses. "Sorry. I don't mean to pry."

He looked up as the waiter returned with their drinks.

Once he'd gone, Diego held out his glass to her.

"What are we drinking to?" she asked.

Jeez, that smile could persuade her of pretty much anything if she wasn't careful. At least, she thought so, until she heard his next words.

"New beginnings."

She set her glass down and shook her head.

"No? Why? We drank to it earlier."

She met his gaze. "For Audrey—and maybe for her and Ted."

He set his glass down. "Not for you? Not for me?"

She shook her head. "I'll drink to a new beginning for you if you have one in mind."

He looked puzzled. "I don't understand you, Izzy."

She smiled. "Well, then let me lay it out for you. Of course, I find you attractive. But no, I have no interest in beginning anything with you."

There went that damned smirk again. "So, even if Ted and Audrey start seeing each other—your best friend and mine—you're saying that this will not be the beginning of a friendship between you and me?"

She made a face. "You know damned well what I meant."

He sighed. "I do. I'm sorry. You confuse me. If I go by your words, I should back off and treat you as a sister."

"So, why don't you?" Much as the thought dampened the excitement that was rushing through her veins, it would be the sensible solution.

He raised an eyebrow at her. "Because if I go by your actions—and your reactions to me—I should ignore your words and take you upstairs."

She wanted to act offended, but she couldn't. It was a fair assessment. "Well, a gentleman always takes a lady at her word."

He nodded. "And I am a gentleman."

"I don't doubt it."

She had to laugh when he winked and added, "Especially in bed."

She slapped his arm. "Damn. I bet your little black book is full of willing women just waiting on your call, isn't it?"

He smiled but didn't answer the question. Instead, he raised an eyebrow. "What about you? Do you have a line of eager young things, all waiting and hoping for their chance with the delectable Izzy?"

She shrugged. There wasn't exactly a line of them, but she did have a pool of younger guys she could call when she wanted to go out—or to stay in.

For some reason, it bothered her when he looked disappointed.

"What?" she asked. "What are you looking like that for? It's all right for you to have a bunch of hot young chickies, but not for me?"

He shook his head. "You're a strong, independent woman. I would never criticize your choices. I'm disappointed; that's all."

He was so serious that now Izzy felt disappointed, too. Something in what she'd said had apparently been a deal-breaker for him. "What are you disappointed about?"

"We're different. I won't deny that I have many female friends I can call on—friends who are happy to hear from me. But they're not young *chickies*, as you put it. I'm disappointed because I'm not young, and I get the impression that due to that fact alone, I cannot get my name on your list."

She stared at him for a long moment. He was right, but she felt like a shit admitting it—though, why, she didn't know. "Come on. It's not as though you wanted to be on my list. At best, I was a target of opportunity tonight."

He gave her a rueful smile. "Perhaps you're right. So, shall we leave the subject there and enjoy our drink?"

She smiled, relieved, and lifted her glass to him. "How about to new friends?"

He picked up his glass and tapped it against hers. "New friends."

When he set his glass down, he took hold of her hand. Part of her wanted to pull it away, but it felt like a challenge—and she never backed down from one of those.

"I have a question."

"Ask away." Even as she said it, her heart began to beat faster. If he asked if she wanted to go to his room with him, she'd have a hard time saying no!

"Izzy …"

She swallowed. Here it came. What the hell. Just one night. She'd tried to resist, but apparently, he was irresistible.

He smiled as if he knew what she was thinking—knew that he'd won. "What is it short for?"

She gave him a puzzled look, not understanding the question.

"Is that your full name? Izzy?"

She let out a short laugh. Had that all been in her head?—the way he'd held her hand—the way he'd looked into her eyes? He was looking into them again now, and the gleam in his told her that he knew exactly what he was doing—and the effect he was having on her.

She withdrew her hand from his and reached for her glass. She didn't want to give him the satisfaction of knowing that he'd won—and boy did she need a drink. "No. It's short for Isobel."

"Isobel."

She closed her eyes briefly. It sounded so good the way he said it. Rafa had an accent, too, but he didn't say her name like that. To be fair, he didn't dare call her by her full name anyway.

"Where are you from?"

"I grew up in Colombia if that's what you mean."

"Yeah, sorry. I didn't mean to be rude. It's just you reminded me …" She was hardly going to tell him about Rafa, was she?

He raised an eyebrow.

"Your accent sounds familiar, but different. I know someone from Venezuela."

"I always think that my accent is mostly gone."

"Oh, it is. Mostly. It was just when you said my name."

"Isobel."

She closed her eyes again. When she opened them, he was smiling.

"Miss Isobel. A beautiful name for a beautiful woman."

"Thank you." She truly enjoyed the compliment because she knew he wasn't saying it for her benefit. He was simply rolling the word around and drawing his conclusion.

# Chapter Three

As he walked her toward the elevators, Diego's mind was racing. There was no question that he would love to spend the night with her. He shot a glance at her; no question at all. But there were too many reasons not to. She was attracted to him; he was convinced of it. When he'd leaned in close to her to give her the flower, it had been obvious. But she claimed she wasn't interested. And besides, she wasn't just someone he knew he'd never see again. He had a feeling that Ted was going to be seeing a lot more of Audrey, even after this week. That would likely mean that he would run into Izzy again.

They reached the elevators, and he pressed the button. She turned to look up at him. "What time are you leaving tomorrow?"

He smiled as a thought struck him. "After lunch. And you?"

"The same. I'm riding back to the airport with Ally and Brayden."

He nodded, wondering whether he should suggest it or not.

They stepped inside the elevator when the doors opened. "What floor?"

"I'm on three."

He pressed the button.

"Are you, too?"

He smirked at her. He was, but he wasn't going to tell her that. He wanted to see how she'd react if she thought he was planning on going with her.

She made a face. "We just had our nightcap. You're not getting another one. I'm going to bed."

He smiled and raised an eyebrow.

She laughed. "Alone!"

The doors opened, and she stepped out. "I'm this way," she said and started walking down the hallway.

Diego's room was in the opposite direction, but he went with her.

She laughed again and looked up at him. "It's not happening."

"I'm simply walking you to your room … making sure you get back safely."

"Yeah. Right." She stopped abruptly. "This is me." She leaned back against the door and looked up at him.

There was a smile playing on her lips. He wondered if he should take the risk and move in for a kiss. The signals she was giving off were mixed, to say the least. He rested his hand on the doorframe above her head and leaned closer. Her eyes widened. He knew he could persuade her, but there were too many reasons not to.

"It would seem this is goodbye, Miss Isobel."

He was gratified to see the look of disappointment that crossed her face momentarily. He lowered his head toward her, and when her eyelids drooped, he made his decision. He changed course at the last moment and pecked her cheek before standing back.

Her eyes flew open, and she looked up at him in surprise. She hadn't merely expected him to kiss her; she'd wanted him to. It was obvious. She held his gaze for a moment. "Okay, well, goodnight then. But it won't be goodbye, will it? I mean, I'm sure I'll see you tomorrow … with Audrey and Ted. You know?"

He smiled. It had worked. "It doesn't have to be goodbye if you don't want it to be." He held her gaze and waited.

She gave him a rueful smile. "I'm sure we'll be seeing more of each other."

He let his gaze wander down to her full breasts, and she laughed and slapped his arm.

"I don't mean like that! I mean, because your best friend and mine look as though they're going to start seeing each other, so it's inevitable …"

He chuckled as he looked at her breasts again. "I believe it is."

She pursed her lips. "Inevitable that we'll run into each other again, even after tomorrow. Not what you're thinking."

"What am I thinking?"

She shook her head. "You know damned well what I mean. You're not going to make me say it."

"Very well. Then I'll be good. I'll bid you goodnight."

She nodded. She still wanted him to kiss her. He knew it, but he didn't do it. He used it to his advantage instead. "Would you like me to give you a ride home tomorrow?"

She frowned. "I'm riding with Ally and Brayden to the airport."

"It's a long drive, and then you'll have to deal with the hassle at the airport. Wouldn't you rather fly with me?"

She raised an eyebrow.

"The jet's at the private airfield right here in Summer Lake. I can have you home before Ally and Brayden even get to the airport."

She held his gaze for a moment, and he wondered if she was about to turn him down. She wasn't the type to be impressed by talk of a private jet, he could tell. It was one of many things he liked about her. "Okay, thanks."

He felt himself relax. "Great." He took out his phone. "Do you want to give me your number? I plan to leave after lunch, but I'll call you so we can make arrangements."

He tapped in the number as she told it to him, then closed his phone with a smile. "Very well, Miss Isobel. I'll see you tomorrow." He leaned toward her again, knowing that this time she expected the kiss. Instead, he put his hands on her waist and drew her closer as he pecked her cheek. "Goodnight."

"Goodnight." She looked stunned as he stepped away from her.

He had to force himself to turn and walk away.

~ ~ ~

Izzy let herself into her room and then leaned back against the door. She took big, deep breaths to steady herself. Damn! She'd been sure that he was coming inside with her—convinced he was going to kiss her. And then he hadn't! She didn't get it. Did she have it all wrong? She'd put money on him wanting to sleep with her. But he'd had two opportunities to make his move, and he hadn't.

She pushed away from the door and went to the minibar. He'd gotten to her. He might not be her type ... she let out a short laugh. Who was she trying to kid? He was gorgeous! She couldn't claim that she wasn't attracted to tall, dark, muscular, handsome men. Only that she preferred to avoid them.

She took her drink out onto the balcony. Even that wasn't true. Rafa was tall, dark, and handsome—muscular, too. He was a personal trainer. He had the physique. So, what was it about Diego that put her off? She sat down and put her feet up on the little coffee table and looked out at the moonlight reflecting off the lake. It wasn't his looks, that was for sure. It wasn't even his presence—if that was the right word for it. He was one of those larger-than-life kind of guys who just had a powerful presence.

She pursed her lips. She was getting closer to the truth now—powerful. She didn't like that. It was attractive, sure. But it wasn't something she wanted to get too close to. Who was she trying to kid? Outside the door just now, she'd been all about getting closer to him. When he'd leaned in to kiss her, she'd felt her knees go weak. Then when he'd pulled her in to kiss her cheek before he left? She'd wanted nothing more than to close her arms around him and move in closer still.

She blew out a sigh. Was he just toying with her? She got the feeling he was, and she didn't like it. She wanted more, but she didn't like feeling that she was the mouse and he was the cat, finding some amusement in teasing her before he moved in for the kill.

She sat there for a while, wondering what tomorrow might hold. He had her off balance, no two ways about it. She wasn't sure if he'd offered her a ride home just to try to impress her with the fact that he had a private jet, or if he planned to play with her some more. She got up to go back inside with a wry smile on her face. The idea of playing with him was appealing. But she shouldn't. She didn't get involved with guys with big egos. She'd do well to stick with Rafa. He was sweet. He was straightforward. He was great in bed! It wasn't as though they were exclusive or anything. He'd started making noises about wanting more lately, but she'd been clear with him from the start. They weren't going anywhere. Theirs was a purely physical relationship.

She took her time getting ready for bed. She wished she felt more tired, but her mind was still busy, and her body was still on high alert. She had a sneaking suspicion that Diego had deliberately left her wanting him.

Or was she crazy? What exactly had he done? He'd pecked her cheek … that was all. See, this was why she avoided men like him. She got herself all wound up. She'd do better to forget all about him. Get some sleep and tomorrow go home, maybe get a workout with Rafa—and not in the gym.

# Chapter Four

Zack glanced over at Diego.

"What?"

"Nothing."

Diego smiled. "It's obvious that you have a question, *mi hijo*. Go ahead. Ask."

"I know it's none of my business, but I'm curious about this woman you're taking home."

Diego chuckled. "I'm not taking her home. Only giving her a ride. And to be clear—I did not take her home last night."

Zack laughed. "So, you keep insisting. And if anything, that's what has me so curious. You've never hidden the fact that you take women home. I'm not judging, you know that. So why are you making such a big deal of the fact that this is different?"

Diego frowned. Why was he? "Perhaps it's because this is about Ted. Not about me. Izzy is Audrey's friend. Ted and Audrey hit it off last night. I am merely—"

Zack laughed. "You don't need to justify it to me, you know."

"I know. I wasn't justifying. I was explaining … because you're so curious."

They drove on in silence for a little while. Diego had had breakfast with Zack and Maria this morning, and now they were on the way to the Boathouse to collect Izzy.

"I'm glad Ted's staying for a while," said Zack.

Diego nodded. He'd been surprised when Ted had announced last night that he wasn't coming home today. He shouldn't have been, though. Ted loved spending time here with his son and his grandson. Apparently, Marcus had asked if he would stay for the week, and Ted was happy to. It couldn't have worked out better since Audrey was also here for the week.

"Is there any chance you might get a week up here soon?"

He looked over at Zack. "Any time you like. You say the word, and I'll be here." More and more lately, Diego had wished that he got to spend more time here with Zack and his fiancée, Maria. There had been too many years when he hadn't seen much of Zack. Now that the danger was behind them, he would love to make up for lost time. But he didn't want to invite himself into their lives more than he was welcome.

Zack smiled at him as he brought the truck to a stop in the square at the resort. "Well, then, here's the word. I'd love to see as much of you as I can. Any time you can spare, I—we—would love for you to come up here. I know it's not easy with work and everything."

"It's as easy as I want to make it. You must know you're more important to me."

Zack nodded. "I do. I just don't want to ask too much."

Diego reached across and grasped his son's shoulder. "That would be impossible. I'm the one who doesn't want to impose too much."

"That's what would be impossible, Dad. We lost so many years. I want us to make up for that. I want you to be part of our lives."

Diego's heart expanded in his chest, filled with love for his son. "I would love nothing more. From now on, I'll be here whenever I'm not working."

Zack laughed. "You mean whenever you're not working or entertaining a lady friend or two?"

Diego smiled through pursed lips. "I will not deny that I like the ladies. But there are ladies here, too."

Zack raised an eyebrow. "And one in particular. Does she come up here much? Is this someone who ...?" He let the question trail off, but Diego knew he was asking whether Izzy might be someone who he might see again here and at home.

He shrugged. "I told you. I only met her last night. I'm only giving her a ride home because ..." He paused to wonder again why he'd offered.

Zack laughed. "It's okay. I know why. You're taking her home today because you didn't take her home last night."

"Perhaps."

They made their way out onto the deck of the restaurant. He spotted Ted, who looked as though he and his family had just finished lunch. He scanned the other tables and soon spotted Izzy sitting with Audrey and her family. He felt his pulse quicken at the sight of her. Last night, she'd been dressed to kill in a low-cut dress that had left him finding it hard to drag his eyes away from her ample breasts. Today she looked much more casual in jeans and a black shirt. Casual as her outfit might be, she still took his breath away.

Zack turned and raised an eyebrow at him but didn't say anything.

Ted hadn't seen them approach, and he jumped when Diego put his hand on his shoulder. "I thought I'd find you here. I'm almost ready to leave."

"Do you want to come and say goodbye to Audrey before you go—and Izzy?"

Diego chuckled. "I'm on my way to bid the lovely Audrey farewell."

Ted raised an eyebrow. "Not Izzy?" The look on his face told Diego he had questions about what might have happened last night.

He couldn't help but smile, knowing that this would only raise further questions. "Not yet. I'm giving her a ride home."

"I see."

"No. You don't. It's just a ride."

"Which you offered out of the goodness of your heart and not in the hope of impressing her by taking her in your private jet?"

"Ted, Ted." Diego chuckled. "When will you understand that when I wish to impress a woman, I don't use the jet?"

Zack laughed beside him. "It's true. You know it's true."

"Okay. But I don't think we need to discuss what you do use—not in front of a lady." Ted gave his son's fiancée, April, an apologetic smile, but she just laughed.

"I'm going to talk to Ally. I'm staying out of this."

Diego was happy to follow her across the deck to where Izzy was sitting with Audrey's family. She smiled when she saw him.

Diego hadn't had the chance to catch up with Ted this morning to ask how things had gone with Audrey, but he got the impression that they'd gone very well. Ted smiled at Audrey's ex-husband as he pecked her cheek. "We're leaving, and I wanted to say goodbye to Ally and Brayden."

Diego saw an evil look flash in the ex-husband's eyes. He didn't want any trouble starting here, so he spoke up, too. "And I have come to tell Miss Isobel that her chariot awaits whenever she is ready."

Ted and Audrey both turned to see what Izzy's reaction would be.

"Can you call it a chariot when it has wings?" she asked.

Ally grinned at Diego. "You're flying her home?"

"I could hardly leave her behind."

Izzy met his gaze when he said that. He could tell that he'd done right to leave her on her doorstep last night. She was more receptive to him now. Perhaps, when they landed in Ventura, he would take her home and finish what they'd started. He smirked and raised an eyebrow at her.

The way she smiled back at him said that she might be as interested in that idea as he was.

Izzy looked out of the window as the plane thundered down the runway and up into the sky. The lake shimmered beneath them in the afternoon sun. Her breath caught in her chest as Diego leaned closer—ostensibly to look out of the window, but she'd put money on the fact that he knew the effect his closeness had on her and was using it to his advantage.

She turned to look up into his eyes. He was so incredibly handsome. She had to ask herself what the harm would be in letting him take advantage. His smile told her that he must know her resolve was weakening. The lines around his eyes deepened as he chuckled. The sound seemed to reverberate through her body.

"Thank you for allowing me to take you home."

She laughed. "Thank you for wanting me to come."

He raised one eyebrow, and that smirk was both enticing and infuriating at the same time. "Oh, I want you to come, Miss Isobel."

Her heart leapt into her mouth. So, he was stepping it up a notch, was he? She held his gaze for a long moment.

"Yet, still, I'm not sure that you want to come with me."

She pursed her lips; she knew what he meant, but she wasn't going to answer—not least because she still wasn't sure what her answer was. Of course, she'd love to come with him. What woman in her right mind wouldn't? But she was still wary. She didn't get involved with guys like him—not even for the sort of brief encounter he had in mind.

He was still holding her gaze, waiting for her to speak.

"I'm here, aren't I?"

He smiled. "But that still doesn't answer my question."

She laughed. "It's probably a bad idea."

"Why?"

"Because of Audrey and Ted. I think they're going to be seeing a lot more of each other. Which means that we probably will, too."

He chuckled. "That's my point."

Shivers chased each other down her spine as his leg brushed against hers.

"I'd like to see a lot more of you."

She let out an exasperated laugh. "Let it go, Diego, would you? You win. Yes, you're an attractive man. Yes, I'm attracted to you. But no, I don't think we should sleep together because our best friends just got together. I think they might be onto something—something special—and they're going to need our support."

"I agree that we must support our friends. But why would us sleeping together interfere with that?"

She pursed her lips. "Because …" She had to ask herself the same question before she could answer. Then it hit her, and she understood. "Because between you and me, it would be a one and done."

"You don't know that."

She laughed. "I'd put money on it."

He gave her a mock hurt look. "You'd have to try me before you decide that you don't want more."

She had to laugh. He was so damned arrogant. "Well, I can tell you that you *would* want more."

That was a mistake. She'd risen to the bait, and now he was smiling, letting his leg brush against hers. "I believe you."

She put her hand on his arm. "Can we drop this? It's not going to happen, okay?"

He lifted a shoulder and held her gaze for a long moment. "If you say so."

The pilot's voice came over the speakers. "We've reached cruising altitude, and ATC tell me we're in for a smooth ride. You can unbuckle now. I'll let you know when you need to strap back in."

Diego unfastened his seat belt and got to his feet. "Can I get you a drink?"

"Please."

~ ~ ~

When the plane touched down on the runway in Ventura, Diego looked out of the window. He knew that this could be goodbye, and he didn't want it to be. It wasn't just that Izzy was such an attractive woman; he could go home and call several of those—any one of whom would be happy to come over and spend a Sunday afternoon and night with him. There was something more to Izzy. She was a challenge, yes, but there was more even than that. She made out she was a tough cookie, but there was a softness, too. He remembered the pain in her eyes last night when she'd spoken of how she hadn't been able to have children.

Karl's voice came over the speaker. "I'll have you to the FBO building in just a few minutes. The car is waiting outside."

Izzy raised an eyebrow at Diego. "The car?"

"I asked Karl to arrange one. You don't think I'd just drop you here and leave you to fend for yourself, do you?"

She smiled. "Thank you."

"It's my pleasure." He winked at her. "I could ride with you to make sure that you get home okay."

She held his gaze for a long moment. When he was almost sure that she was about to refuse, she laughed.

"Okay, then. Why not? You got me home hours earlier than I expected to be here. I have no plans for the afternoon. Why don't you come with me?"

He gave her a questioning look. Was she using the same wordplay that he had earlier?

She gave him a sassy smile, and his heart started to race. He could think of nothing he would rather do with his afternoon than spend it in bed with her. They'd teased each other last night and this morning—that was a protracted courtship as far as he was concerned.

He pressed the button on the arm of his chair and spoke to Karl. "You might want to refuel and then go get yourself some lunch. Maybe go to see the beach." He smiled at Izzy. "I'm going to be a while."

Butterflies swirled in Izzy's stomach when he said that. What had she done? She'd almost managed to survive this infuriatingly sexy man without succumbing to his charms. All she'd needed to do was thank him for arranging a car for her and then go. Why hadn't she?

As he held her gaze and told the pilot that he was going to be a while, it couldn't be clearer why she hadn't. No matter how big or macho or full-on he might be, he was irresistible. He might be the kind of guy that she didn't go for, but she couldn't deny that he was worth making an exception for. All the muscles in her stomach and lower tightened when he reached over and unfastened her seat belt for her as the plane came to a halt.

She was surprised to find her hand shaking when she put the key in the lock in her front door. She wanted to believe that she was shaking with excitement, not nerves.

Diego's hand came down on her shoulder, and a rush of heat spread through her. "Do I make you nervous?"

When she turned and looked up into his eyes, she almost told him that what he made her was horny. But she thought better of it. An ego like his didn't need that kind of boost. Instead, she pushed the door open and gestured for him to go in ahead of her.

He waited just inside the door, and when she closed it again, he stepped toward her.

It wasn't as though she was some shy retiring little thing who'd never brought a guy home and started tearing his clothes off in the hallway before, but when she had, she'd been the one calling the shots. Diego was different.

She stepped away from him and hurried to the kitchen. "Would you like a drink?"

He raised an eyebrow.

"Wine, beer, water, something stronger?" Right now, she could use a shot of the strong stuff herself, though why he was having this effect on her, she just didn't know.

He took a seat at the island. "I'll take a water."

She filled two glasses of iced water and set one down in front of him. As she brought hers to her lips to take a drink, the ice cubes tinkled against the glass, giving away just how nervous she was.

Diego took a drink and then set his glass down. He got to his feet, and for the first time, she realized just how much he towered over her. "Do I make you uncomfortable?"

She shook her head.

"What's going on then, Miss Isobel?"

She looked up into his big brown eyes, asking herself the same thing. What was going on? She was no stranger to bringing guys home. She didn't see anything wrong with it. It was no big deal in her mind. So, why, with Diego, did it feel so … so much like a big deal? She finally admitted to herself.

"I don't know." She gave him a wry smile. "I'm surprised at myself."

He put his hands on her shoulders and then ran them down her arms until they cupped her elbows. He drew her toward him, and she went willingly.

She looked up into his eyes. Over the course of last night and this morning, she'd seen them gleam with mischief, tease her with temptation, and twinkle with amusement. Now, she was shocked to see them filled with—tenderness? That couldn't be right. Concern maybe?

He cocked his head to one side. "I'd like to get to know you, Miss Isobel."

For a moment, it seemed as though he was talking about something more than physically. But no. He couldn't mean that—and if he did, she couldn't allow herself to go anywhere near it. She laughed. "You mean in the biblical sense?"

He shook his head and brought his mouth closer to hers. The feel of him so close made her forget everything. Her arms acted of their own accord and reached up around his neck. Her knees went weak as he pulled her against his chest. And her mind lost its grip on reality when his lips came down on hers.

Damn, the man could kiss! She felt dazed when he finally lifted his head and smiled down at her.

"Give me one good reason why we shouldn't get to know each other better." His smile was gentle and even sexier than before when he added, "And not just in the biblical sense.

Perhaps Ted and Audrey aren't the only ones who have found something special."

Her heart pounded in her chest. Of all the things she'd expected him to say, that wasn't one of them. She'd expected something charming, or sexy, some kind of line to persuade her into bed. Not that kind of talk. She stepped away from him hurriedly.

"One good reason?"

He nodded, looking wary now.

"Well, I should have been honest with you earlier. I'm seeing someone."

His eyebrows knit together. She wouldn't have expected him to be the kind of guy who cared about that sort of thing, but the look on his face told her that he did. "Who is he?"

She shrugged. "I know him from the gym." She and Rafa weren't exactly a couple, but they had been screwing each other for a couple of months.

"I see. And it's serious?"

She laughed at the thought, but then stopped. She'd have to say it was some kind of serious if she was using Rafa as an excuse not to sleep with Diego. "Sort of."

He held her gaze, and for some reason, she felt bad for lying to him.

"If you must know, he's my trainer."

Her heart sank at the way his expression changed. "How old is he?"

She shrugged. "What does it matter?"

"I'm curious. I'd like to know."

"He's thirty-seven."

Diego nodded and looked at his watch. "I should go."

"You don't have to." She felt bad now. Bad that she seemed to have ruffled his feathers by telling him that she was seeing someone younger—and worse, that for some reason she'd screwed this up and wasn't going to get to spend the afternoon in bed with him after all.

He blew out a sigh and gave her a sad smile. "I think we both know that it's for the best." He took hold of her hand and brought it up to his lips. The feel of them on her skin as he brushed them over her wrist made her want to kick herself for not having kept her mouth shut.

"My apologies. I hope you and your trainer will be very happy together. I'm sure I'll see you again—I hope for Ted and Audrey's sake that I do. But, in the future, I shall behave appropriately."

She followed him to the door, wishing that she'd handled this differently. She watched him get into the rental car. He met her gaze one last time and gave her a rueful smile before he drove away.

She closed the door and went back inside to pour herself a stiff drink. She laughed as she did, remembering how he'd told her last night that he could help her if she needed a stiff one. How she wished she'd let him!

She knew that later she'd be glad that she hadn't succumbed to his charms; it was for the best. She didn't date—or even screw—guys like him. Later, she'd be proud of herself, but right now, she was only disappointed.

# Chapter Five

"Are you going to fly up with us this weekend?" asked Ted.

"No. I plan to leave this evening."

"Oh. Why's that?"

"I have an appointment with Austin tomorrow—the realtor."

"You're serious about getting yourself a place up there, then?"

Diego smiled. "I am."

"Isn't it amazing how much can change in just a couple of weeks?"

"It might only have been a couple of weeks, but I'd say all of this has been brewing for a long time. You meeting Audrey was just the catalyst for changes that were waiting to happen."

"You're right."

"Aren't I always?"

Ted laughed. "What do you say? Do you want to get dinner together? Who knows when we'll get the chance to do it again."

Diego nodded. "Let's go, but don't say things like that. You'll make me cry." He was only half-joking. So much had changed in the couple of weeks since Ted had met Audrey.

They were all good changes. He knew that, but it did make him feel a little sentimental to think that this era of their lives—the one where he and Ted lived here in Laguna Beach and went into the office every day—was coming to an end.

Ted grasped his arm. "In the future, we'll have dinner together at the Boathouse. That's all."

"I know. But this …" He swept his arm around the boardroom, where they were still sitting long after the meeting had finished. "This life we built here, it's coming to an end, no?"

Ted nodded. "Kind of. It's not ending, but it'll be taking a back seat to everything new we have going on."

"To your new life with your new lady. Do you think things will work out at the lake for them this weekend?"

"I hope so."

Much had happened in the couple of weeks since Ted and Audrey had met. Her first week at the lake with Ted had been cut short when her son had had an accident, and they'd come rushing back to Ventura to take care of him. Since then, they'd become very much a couple, and it had pissed her ex off to no end. He'd meddled in her kids' lives, costing them both their jobs, and Ted was bringing them to the lake this weekend to help them find work there.

Diego had supported his friend through a crazy couple of weeks, and in the process, he'd made some decisions about his own life. Coming in here to the office every day while Ted was gone had made him realize that he didn't want to be here. The bank had been his life for more years than he cared to remember. But after his conversation with Zack about spending more time together, he was ready to make some changes.

This weekend, Ted was taking Audrey and her kids to Summer Lake to help them start a new life there. And he was going to start house hunting. There was no reason for him or Ted to come in here every day anymore. It was time to make the move.

Ted was watching him with a smile playing on his lips.

"What?"

"You haven't asked about Izzy."

Diego's heart thudded at the mention of her name. It always did. Ted had talked about her a few times over the last couple of weeks. He knew he'd have to hear about her. Knew he'd have to run into her up at the lake at some point, but he'd made his decision. He wasn't going to make any more attempts to pursue her. It was for the best. "What should I be asking?"

Ted laughed. "Whether she's coming this weekend."

Diego closed his eyes, briefly remembering their conversation about her coming with him. He forced himself to focus. That wouldn't be happening. That was what she did with her trainer—her much younger trainer. He'd never thought that his fifty-seven years on this earth were a disadvantage in any respect. He knew that older meant wiser, and he was in great shape. But when it came to Izzy, his age was his downfall. He should have admitted it from the outset when he'd heard her say how hot Ted's son was.

"Are you all right?"

He'd forgotten that Ted was waiting for an answer. He shrugged. "I didn't think she would be. I thought that this was about you and Audrey and Ally and Brayden."

"It is." Ted smiled. "And I was wondering if you might want to keep Izzy company if Audrey and I get tied up with other things."

"I wouldn't worry about her. She's not someone who needs a man to take care of her. And besides, if she's looking for company, she'd probably prefer you asked one of Eddie's friends."

Ted laughed. "She got to you, didn't she?"

"I told you. My ego took a bit of a hit. But …" He shrugged. "I'm over it."

"So, will you be okay to hang out with her?"

"Of course. It's behind us. Forgotten. I'm your best friend. She's Audrey's." He smiled. "It's all okay."

Ted looked relieved. "Good. I'm glad to hear it."

"You know I wouldn't make things difficult for you."

"Of course, I do. I was more concerned about how you would feel about it."

Diego laughed. "You think I would be upset about a woman? When have you ever known me to do that?"

"Never. But …" Ted held his gaze for a moment. "I get the feeling there's something different about Izzy—about you and Izzy."

Diego looked back at him. He kept getting that feeling himself. But it was ridiculous, and apart from that, it was irrelevant. Izzy wasn't interested in him. There was no point in him being interested in her.

~ ~ ~

Izzy made herself a cup of coffee and took it out onto the balcony. She hadn't expected to come back to Summer Lake this soon, but she was glad to be here. It was a great place. The lake was beautiful, as were the mountains.

She took a sip of her coffee and sat down. She couldn't help but remember the last time she'd sat out on her balcony here—after she'd said goodnight to Diego. She got goose bumps just thinking about it. How could the man still have that effect on her? It wasn't right.

She'd been so dumb to turn him down when he'd taken her home after their last visit here. He'd asked her for one good reason why they shouldn't sleep together, and she'd told him she was seeing Rafa! It hadn't been a good enough reason at the time, and now it was no longer a reason at all. Rafa had come around that same afternoon not long after Diego had left.

She'd had to wonder what she'd ever seen in him. No. That wasn't fair. She knew exactly what she saw in him; he was a good-looking guy with a great body. He was fun and … compared to Diego he was … nothing. He was a sweet guy, but he didn't have Diego's confidence or sense of fun. There was nothing magnetic about his personality or his … presence. She kept coming back to that word whenever she thought about Diego. There was just something about him. When he was there, you knew he was there. He filled up the room—he filled up her senses if she cared to admit it.

She blew out a sigh and took another sip of her coffee. She was expecting to run into him today. Apparently, he was staying here at the lodge again, too. She'd expected that he'd be flying up here with them yesterday; she'd steeled herself for that, planning to be fun and flirty with him—to keep up their initial banter and hope that he would go along with it.

It'd turned out she hadn't needed to worry about sitting next to him on the plane. Ted told her that he'd come up on Thursday because he was house hunting. The realization hit her that he would probably move up here, and so would Audrey and Ted at some point. Diego would still get to be an everyday part of his best friend's life while she was going to lose Audrey.

She felt bad, even thinking it. It was a selfish thought, and it wasn't like her. She was thrilled for her friend. She really was.

Even now, though, she knew that things were changing— and it was only as it should be. Last time they'd been here, Izzy had called Audrey first thing and gone to her room to chat before they went down for breakfast. Today, she wouldn't call her. She didn't want to intrude on her time with Ted. The two of them would be waking up together and would eat together when they were ready.

She picked up her cup and took it back inside. She'd have a shower and then go down to get some breakfast by herself.

Diego buttered a croissant and scrolled through his emails. He was looking forward to today. Austin had three houses lined up for him to look at. He couldn't wait to have his own place here. He'd had dinner with Zack and Maria last night, and when the conversation had somehow turned to babies, he'd learned that they were eager to start their family once they were married. The thought of grandbabies made his eyes fill with tears. He couldn't wait! He'd love to be a grandpa, and he wanted to be a part of their lives in a real way—by living here, not by showing up on the weekends and coming over for barbecues on Saturday afternoon.

He looked around the dining room. It was getting busier now. He'd come down early and taken his time, but he should get going, free up his table. He started to get to his feet and then sat back down again when he saw her.

Isobel. He'd known he'd run into her this weekend. His heart raced in his chest as he watched her. He'd tried to convince himself in the last couple of weeks that she wasn't that special. Tried to tell himself that he'd let a great set of breasts turn his head. He smiled. He wasn't wrong about that part—her breasts drew his eye again this morning. But above them, her face was so beautiful. The rest of her was just … breathtaking. Not in a physically perfect way, there was something more to her than that. She seemed to bounce along, filled with good energy. He watched as she smiled at the woman beside her and let her go ahead of her.

She took her time getting cereal and fruit and coffee. Then she turned to look around the room, searching for a place to sit. He resisted the urge to raise his hand and wave her over. He wanted to, but instead, he chose to wait—to see what she'd do if she saw him.

He was rewarded when her gaze met his. Her eyes widened in recognition. He relaxed when she smiled and started making her way over to him.

"Hi. Do you mind if I join you? It's busy in here."

He smiled through pursed lips. "You only want me for my table?"

She held his gaze for a long moment and then laughed. "I want so much more from you than that."

His heart leaped in his chest, but he got a grip quickly. He had to remember that when he'd been offering more, she'd turned him down—in favor of her young boyfriend.

He raised an eyebrow, and she laughed again and picked up a packet of butter from his plate. "I want this, too."

He had to laugh with her. She'd won that point.

"So, how have you been?" She was friendly, bright, and breezy—and judging by the way her nipples were pointing at him through her blouse, she was still interested in him, no matter what she might say.

He gave her a sad smile. "Heartbroken, but I struggle on."

She stopped with her spoon mid-air and looked at him. Then she                                        laughed. "You're so full of it."

He gave her another sad look. "You turn me down. You break my heart. And then you tell me that I'm full of it?"

"Because you are."

He shrugged. "I have been well, thank you. And you? How have you and your boyfriend been? Is he with you?"

She pursed her lips. "He isn't."

Diego got the impression that he didn't go anywhere with her. But he decided against asking. He was still enjoying playing with her, but he didn't want to risk having her tell him that actually, things with her trainer boyfriend were serious.

"Anyway. How about you? I hear you're moving up here?"

"I'm looking for a house here. I want to be close to my boy." He smiled. "I want to be here for when they start their family, you know?"

His heart sank when he saw her expression. Of course, she didn't know. She couldn't. She didn't have children. And so, she would never know how wonderful it would be to have grandchildren. He couldn't help it. He reached across the table and took hold of her hand. "I'm sorry. That was insensitive of me."

She gave him a bright smile, but it didn't reach her eyes. "Not a problem. It's just not something I can relate to."

"I'm sorry."

"Don't be. I'm happy for you."

"Thank you." Part of him wanted to ask if she wanted to come house hunting with him. He didn't like to think of her at a loose end while Ted and Audrey did their thing.

She removed her hand from his, and he thought better of asking. What was he thinking? She wasn't interested in him. He'd do better to stay out of her way. Being around her made him want more, and she couldn't have been clearer that she wasn't interested.

He checked his watch. He needed to get going soon anyway. He had to drive around to the other side of the lake to meet Austin. He was going to look at houses in town, on the water, near Zack.

He reached for her hand again, and she let him take it. This time he brought it to his lips. He almost kissed the back of it, but curiosity made him turn it over. Last time he'd seen her, she hadn't been able to hide the way it turned her on when he'd kissed her wrist. He did it again, brushing his lips against her skin in the lightest touch. He was thrilled to see her eyes widen, and a touch of color appear in her cheeks. He didn't miss the way her breasts rose and fell as she took a deep breath.

He smiled to himself. Her boy toy trainer might get to be the one to sleep with her, but he wasn't enough to stop her from reacting to the touch of another man—a real man.

She looked up into his eyes as he got to his feet. "It's time we must say goodbye again, Miss Isobel."

She nodded. She didn't want him to go; he could tell. And that made him happy. Much happier than it should.

~ ~ ~

By lunchtime on Sunday, Izzy was more than ready to go home. It had been a great weekend. She knew that she'd look back on it as a turning point in her life. Ted had proposed to Audrey. Izzy was thrilled for her friend. It might be fast, but Izzy really didn't think that mattered. Ted was perfect for her, and it wasn't like they were planning to get married straight away, just engaged—and move in together. Ally and Brayden had both found work up here, and it only made sense that Audrey would want to be here, too. Ted's family was already here.

She looked across the lobby to where Diego had just emerged from the elevator. He'd found himself a house that he'd fallen in love with. All of them were going to be moving here. All except her.

She gave herself a little shake. She was happy for her friend. Happy for the kids. Hell, she was happy for Ted and Diego, too. They were both good guys who were embarking on the next chapter of their lives. It sounded as though they'd worked hard for years to build a bank—it sounded more like an empire to her when they talked about it. And now they were ready to start taking it a bit easier, spending more time here with their families.

She forced herself to smile. That was what really hurt. They were all moving to be closer to their families. She was going to be left behind, and she didn't even have a family.

Nope. She wasn't going there.

She smiled when Brayden came to sit down beside her. They were waiting in the lobby of the lodge for a minibus that would take them all back to the airport.

"Did you have a good weekend, Aunt Izzy?"

"I did, Bray. Are you excited about your new job?"

He grinned. "I can't wait to get started. It's going to be awesome. Don't you think? I mean, living up here will be different from the beach, but I think I'm going to love it. Do you?"

"I'm sure you will."

"No, I mean, don't you think you're going to love it, too?"

"I won't be coming here."

He frowned at her. "What? What do you mean? You … you have to. Mom's going to be moving up here with Ted. How are you guys going to run the agency if you're not here?"

She smiled. "We'll work online. We were behind the times if you think about it. There's no need for us to go into the office every day. No reason to actually be in the same physical space."

Brayden frowned. "Maybe not for work. But you two are best friends. You have to be in the same place. You always have been."

She shrugged. "Things change, Bray." She nodded toward where Audrey was standing with Ted. His arm was slung around her shoulders as they talked with Diego. "Ted's going to be her best friend now, and that's as it should be."

Brayden frowned at her. "I don't like it, Aunt Iz. I want you to move up here with us. Life won't be the same without you."

She managed to blink away the tears before he noticed them. Then she smiled. "That's how it works, Bray. Life doesn't stay the same. It changes, and it moves on."

She jumped when a big hand came down on her shoulder. She knew it was him. Though how he'd gotten behind her was a mystery.

"Are you ready to move on, Miss Isobel?"

Brayden gave her a knowing smile and went to talk to Ally. Izzy steeled herself as she turned around and looked up at Diego. "I'm not going anywhere. You guys are all moving on, moving up here, starting a new chapter of your lives."

"You could do the same." He held her gaze as he spoke. He was getting at something, but she didn't know what. "If you wanted to."

She shook her head and looked out the window at the rain that had been falling for the last couple of hours. The rain always made her feel sad, and today, it was just adding to her sense of loss. She was about to lose Audrey and the kids and her job as she'd known it. She and Audrey had worked in the same office together since college. First, at a big ad agency in LA, then with Audrey's husband, Richard, and for the last few in Audrey's own agency in Ventura.

She looked up at Diego. For all he was the big full-on flirt, he was kind and caring, too. He smiled at her, and for a moment, she wondered what it might be like if the two of them were to get together—for real, not just for sex.

A flash of lightning lit up the sky, followed by the rumble of thunder. It brought her back to her senses. Was she crazy? She shook her head sadly. "It's not in the cards for me."

His smile faded. Suddenly, he seemed as sad as she felt. "I'm sorry you feel that way."

She shrugged. "It is what it is."

"Look!" They both turned to see Ally pointing out the window. "It's a rainbow! Isn't it beautiful?"

Izzy pursed her lips as the others oohed and aahed, and Audrey and Ally took out their phones to take pictures. Even Diego took his out and started snapping away.

He looked down at her. "You don't like rainbows?"

She laughed. "They're pretty enough, but they're no big deal."

He leaned closer, making goose bumps race down her arms. "You don't want to fly with me to the end of the rainbow? See if we can't find the crock of gold?"

She stepped away with a forced laugh. If he was trying to torment her, he was succeeding. She couldn't stay that close to him and not remember the way he'd kissed her—and want more.

"I'll fly back to Ventura with you. But we both know that the only thing waiting at the end of the rainbow is a crock of shit."

His smile disappeared, and she felt bad. She didn't mean to be so cynical, but sometimes she couldn't help it. It seemed that this was one of those times.

# Chapter Six

Izzy looked around the office. Well, it didn't even look like an office anymore. It was just an empty space now. She blew out a sigh and picked up the last box of her belongings: the photo of herself and Audrey at the awards ceremony, the few knick-knacks she'd kept on her desk, the coffeemaker she'd kept here with her until it was time to go. It was the end of an era. She slung her purse strap over her shoulder and headed for the door.

Audrey met her there. "Here, let me take that."

"It's okay. I've got it. Why don't you lock up?"

Audrey put the key in the door and gave her a sad smile. "It's hard to believe that this is the last time we'll do this."

Izzy nodded. "We had some good times here."

Audrey took the key out and tested the door to make sure it was secure. "And we'll have plenty more good times, too. We're giving up the office, Iz. That's all. Nothing else is going to change."

Izzy raised an eyebrow at her.

"You know what I mean. I know lots of things are going to change; they've started to change already, but nothing's going to change between you and me. It never will."

Izzy smiled brightly. She was happy for her friend. She really was. "I know! I was just having a sentimental moment, that's all. Everything's changing for the better. You've got yourself a new man, a new life, the kids are settling in at Summer Lake, and soon you will be, too. It's wonderful."

Audrey held her gaze for a moment. "Are you sure you're okay with it?"

Izzy laughed. "What's not to be okay with? My best friend is happier than I've ever seen her. How could I not be okay with that?"

"I feel like I'm abandoning you."

Izzy rolled her eyes. "Come on. You know I'm going to miss you. I'm going to miss spending our days together here, but you're hardly abandoning me. We're still going to be working together, we'll still see each other every day—it'll just be on a video call instead of in person."

"And we will still see each other in person. You're going to come up to the lake all the time … aren't you?"

"Of course." Even as she said it, Izzy wondered how true that last part was. She would go up and visit, but not all the time. Audrey had Ted now. The two of them needed to build their own life together. She and Audrey had been best friends since high school; they'd seen each other through marriages and divorces—all the highs and lows that stretched over almost forty years of their lives. It was time for her to step back, and she knew it.

If Audrey and Ted were starting their new life here in Ventura, it would be a little different, but they weren't.

Summer Lake was a four-hour drive away. It wasn't as though she and Audrey would still be able to meet up for coffee or a quick lunch. If they wanted to see each other, it would take a big chunk of Audrey's time—whether she came back here, or Izzy went up there—and Izzy didn't want to do that to her.

When they reached the car, Izzy put the box on the back seat.

"Why do I get the feeling that there's something you're not telling me?" asked Audrey.

Izzy shrugged. "I have no idea."

Audrey blew out a sigh.

"It's okay, you're going to be fine."

"I'm not sure if that's true."

Izzy's heart sank. "Why? Has something happened with Ted? I thought you were thrilled with it all."

"I am. He's wonderful. I know I'm going to be okay with him." Her smile told Izzy just how much more than okay they were; the two of them were deeply in love. "I don't know if I can be fine without you in my life, though, Iz."

Izzy felt tears prick behind her eyes and blinked them away rapidly. "Now, you're just being overdramatic. I'm still going to be in your life."

"I know, but it won't be the same."

Izzy gave her a hug. "Of course, it won't; it'll be better, because now you have Ted, too. I think you're just worn out with closing this place down and getting the house packed up. Go on. You go home and get ready. I'll return the keys, and I'll see you at the restaurant."

She stood beside her car as she watched Audrey drive away. If anything, she was more upset about this than Audrey was. She didn't know if she could be fine without her best friend in

her life, but there was no way in hell she was going to tell her
that. Audrey had had such a rough ride for so many years.
Richard was the biggest asshole Izzy had ever known. He'd
made Audrey's life hell. It had taken a few years after the
divorce for her to find her feet again, but now she had Ted. He
might possibly be the nicest guy Izzy had ever met, and he
couldn't be more perfect for Audrey.

Audrey deserved happiness more than anyone, and there was
no way Izzy was going to taint it for her by letting her know
just how sad she was to see her go. Anyway. She gave herself a
shake and got into her car. As she'd said herself, it wasn't as
though they were never going to see each other again. Things
were changing, that was all.

She cast a glance back at the office as she pulled out of the
parking lot. They'd had some good times here, but they'd have
more in the future, too. They weren't closing down. She and
Audrey would still work together, even if it was remotely.

She pulled out into the traffic on her way across town to
return the keys to the leasing agent. After that, she was going
to get her hair done before meeting Audrey for a late lunch. It
was just lunch, that was all. It wasn't a farewell. Even though
they'd just closed up the office for the last time and, after
they'd eaten, Ted would be picking Audrey up and taking her
up to Summer Lake.

She turned the radio on loud and started to sing along. It was
all good.

~ ~ ~

Diego smiled to himself as he stood in the doorway to Ted's
office. He wasn't working; he was sitting staring out the
window with a smile on his face that Diego could tell meant

that he was thinking about Audrey. He'd never known his friend this happy.

He cleared his throat, and Ted spun around in his chair. "Hey!"

Diego chuckled. "Hey. Am I interrupting something important?"

Ted gave him a shamefaced grin. "I was just …"

"Thinking about the lovely Audrey?"

Ted nodded. "Thinking about what we're going to do this weekend."

Diego waggled his eyebrows. "Private thoughts? I can come back."

Ted laughed. "No. Not that. I was thinking about taking her for a hike up on the trails behind the house. We're meeting with Logan on-site to go over the plans, and I want to show her just how far we're going to be able to hike right from our own back door."

"That's good."

"Anyway, what about you? What are your plans for the weekend?"

Diego shrugged. "Zack and Maria are going to see her parents, after all."

"But you're still coming, aren't you?"

He shrugged again. He'd been looking forward to spending the weekend at the lake, but now he wasn't sure.

Ted gave him a puzzled look. "Why not?"

He smiled.

"Do you have a hot date here that I don't know about?"

"No! My son isn't going to be there. I can't get in the house until I close on it—whenever that's going to be. And … if I don't go, you and Audrey will have the plane to yourselves."

"All of that makes sense ... except for the part about you not having a date. You haven't been out on a date in weeks." He gave Diego a curious look. "Months?"

Diego shrugged. "I don't know."

Ted pursed his lips. "I think I know."

"Know what?"

"That you haven't been on a date since I first met Audrey."

Diego laughed. "What are you trying to say?"

"What I'm trying not to say—what I'm hoping that you'll admit—is that you're hung up on Izzy. You met her the same night I met Audrey."

Diego's heart rate picked up. It always did whenever her name came up. "You know me better than that."

Ted raised an eyebrow. "I thought I did, but it's true. You haven't been on a single date since you've known her. That's not like you."

"I've been busy. We've been arranging the business so that we don't have to be here every day. I've been up at the lake trying to speed things up on the house."

Ted gave him a knowing smile. "You're hung up on her, aren't you?"

Diego pursed his lips, but couldn't hold his smile in. "She's a very attractive woman. I have never denied that fact."

"Yeah, but you usually deny that you like her."

He threw his hands in the air. "I have never denied it. But there's no point. She likes younger men, little boys she can push around. That hardly describes me, does it?"

"No, but just because someone has a type doesn't mean that they can't or won't make an exception."

"Perhaps not, but she won't be making one for me."

"Okay. I'll drop it."

Diego almost wished that he wouldn't. They'd had this conversation or some version of it a few times in the last couple of months. He enjoyed considering the possibility of something happening between Izzy and himself, even though he knew that she just wasn't interested.

"What time are you leaving?"

"In a few minutes. Are you really not coming? You know I'm picking Audrey up in Ventura?" He smiled. "She's having lunch with Izzy. I said I'd meet her at the restaurant."

Diego frowned.

"I thought you were coming. I thought you might like to say hello. But ... if you're not interested ..." Ted held his gaze for a long moment.

Diego chuckled. "But if I come with you to Ventura, then I have to go to the lake, too."

"Or ... I could send the plane back for you."

"That's probably a bad idea."

"There's only one way to find out."

Audrey checked her watch, and Izzy smiled.

"Don't worry. He won't be late."

"Sorry. I wasn't thinking about Ted arriving; I was wondering how much time we have left." She looked sad. "I don't like not knowing when we'll get to do this again."

Izzy made a face. "Stop it. We can do it any time you like. And besides, we're going to be talking every day—seeing each other on video chat. It's an adjustment, that's all. We won't be right there with each other, but ..." She smiled. "We'll be right there with each other."

"I know." Audrey turned to look out at the ocean. "Is there any chance you'll come up next weekend?"

"No. I want to give you guys some time to get settled in. I'm sure Ted won't want me around on your first full weekend together ... and I don't blame him."

"This is our first full weekend together."

"You know what I mean. Give it a couple of weeks."

Audrey sighed. "Okay. But you have to promise that you're coming at the end of the month. Clay's going to be singing with the band on the thirtieth."

"In that case, I promise."

Audrey laughed. "You won't come to see me, but you will come to see him sing?"

Izzy waggled her eyebrows. "Sorry, but you don't have the same effect on me that he does. He's gorgeous!"

"Well, if it's going to take a gorgeous man to entice you up there, there's one coming with us this weekend."

Izzy's tummy felt as though it flipped over.

Audrey raised an eyebrow at her. "Your silence speaks volumes."

"I'm surprised, that's all. I thought the two of you were going by yourselves."

"We are ... well, once we get there, we are. But the plane belongs to Diego, too. We're hardly going to fly up there separately."

Izzy nodded slowly. She tried not to let herself think about Diego most of the time. He was one seriously sexy guy. But ...

Audrey gave her a sly smile. "I should probably have warned you that he'll be with Ted when he comes to pick me up."

Izzy's heart leaped into her throat. "Err, yes, you should!"

"Why, though? You claim you're not interested, so why does it matter?"

Izzy rolled her eyes. "I'm not interested, but ..." She laughed. "I've never denied that he's gorgeous."

Audrey tilted her head toward the hostess station with a smile. "Well, if you don't want him to know that's what you think, you might want to shush because they're here."

Izzy resisted the urge to turn and look. She could wait until they came out here onto the terrace where she and Audrey were sitting. Her heart was racing now. She took a sip of her drink, the ice cubes tinkling against the glass as she lifted it.

She smiled as Ted reached them and leaned down to kiss Audrey's cheek. "Hey."

Izzy envied the way her friend smiled at him. There was no mistaking the love in her eyes.

"Izzy." Ted smiled at her.

"Hi, Ted." She could feel Diego standing just behind her. She turned and smiled at him. "Diego." Gorgeous was too small a word for him. He was ... breathtaking. She was used to seeing him dressed casually up at the lake. Right now, he looked as though he'd come straight from the office; he wore a slate gray suit with a crisp white shirt which contrasted against his olive skin.

His smile took her breath away. He took her hand and made a big show of kissing the back of it. "Miss Isobel. It's been too long. You are more beautiful even than I remembered."

It was the briefest touch, but the feel of his lips on her skin sent electric shocks zinging through her. He always had that effect on her, but there was no way she'd let him know it.

Instead, she rolled her eyes at Audrey and Ted. "He's still full of it, then?"

Ted laughed, and Audrey frowned at her.

Diego didn't let go of her hand. He pulled up the seat beside her and turned big brown eyes on her. "Why? Why won't you believe me?"

She laughed. "I say again. You're full of it."

"Do you two want a drink?" asked Audrey.

Ted shot a glance at Izzy that she didn't understand. "If you don't mind, we need to get going. Karl said there's a front coming in, and if we don't get out ahead of it, we'll be stuck here for a while until it blows through."

"Oh." Audrey gave Izzy a sad look. "Are you okay if we go now?"

"Of course. Go on. We're done here anyway."

"I know, but ..."

Izzy hated that her friend was worried about leaving her instead of feeling happy about going off to get started on her new life with Ted. "I'm fine. Honestly. I might sit here and have another drink and enjoy the afternoon."

Diego squeezed her hand and smiled at her. "That's a good idea. You should do that."

He seemed pleased with himself. Though why she didn't know.

"Thanks. I will."

He smirked at her. Damn, she'd forgotten just how sexy that smirk was.

She got to her feet and let Ted peck her cheek before she hugged Audrey. "Just go. Don't make a big deal out of it. I'll talk to you later, okay?"

Audrey nodded. Tears shone in her eyes. Izzy could feel tears of her own burning in her throat. She looked at Ted. "You take care of her, okay?"

"I will. And we'll see you soon? You'll come up and visit?"

She nodded.

Diego took her hand and brought it to his lips again. He held her gaze the whole way. "I will see you very soon, Miss Isobel."

She pressed her lips together and nodded, not trusting herself to speak; her only options were to come out with some put-down or to risk asking him how soon, please?

She let out a sigh as she watched the three of them walk away. A chapter of her life was ending; she knew it. But she also knew that a new and better one was starting for Audrey, and that made it all worthwhile.

# Chapter Seven

After they'd gone, Izzy picked up her glass and drained it. It was nice out here. The sun shone brightly, but the terrace was shady and cool. She pursed her lips. She'd told Audrey that she might sit here a while. When she'd said it, it was just to reassure her friend that she'd be fine. But now that she thought about it, she realized that she may as well; she had nothing else to do with her afternoon.

She fiddled with her glass. She could go to the gym and get a workout in, but she didn't really feel like it. It was Friday afternoon, which meant Rafa would be working. If she went in, he'd probably think that she was there for him. She smiled. She had enjoyed the workouts that they used to give each other. But it had been a while, and he didn't hold the same appeal anymore.

She turned to see if she could catch the waiter's eye. She might as well order a drink as sit here thinking about it.

She did a double take when a guy who looked a lot like Diego came out onto the terrace. He smiled at her, and her heart started to race, confirming that it was, in fact, him and not just some look alike.

"What are you doing back?" She looked past him, wondering where Audrey and Ted were.

He pulled up the seat beside her and held her gaze, making her breath catch in her chest. "I told you I would see you very soon."

She didn't understand. "What's going on? Where are they?"

"They're on their way to Summer Lake."

She frowned. "And you? You're not going?"

His lips quirked up into that smirk. "I am not. I couldn't stand to think of you sitting here all alone." He reached for her hand, and she was too confused to pull it away. "May I keep you company?"

She searched his face. He wasn't joking.

The waiter came over, and Diego raised an eyebrow at her. "The same again?"

She nodded, still struggling to process what was going on.

When the waiter had gone, Diego squeezed her hand. She met his gaze, and he looked deep into her eyes. Oh, he was good. He probably had women falling at his feet with that move. She wriggled in her seat, wondering briefly why she shouldn't be one of them.

The hint of a smile touched his lips, and she'd bet that he knew the effect he was having on her. She withdrew her hand.

"Are you afraid of me, Miss Isobel?"

She laughed. "Afraid? Why would I be afraid?"

He let his gaze travel over her, and she felt a rush of heat sweep through her and settle between her legs. Damn. He was good at this game. "I was hoping you'd tell me."

"I'm not afraid of you, Diego. I'm just wise to you and your ways."

His smile was confident, to say the least. "What are my ways?"

"You know what I mean. You expect me to fall for your lines and your good looks. I'm not afraid. I'm just not interested. I've told you before."

He leaned toward her and rested his hand on her knee, making her close her eyes briefly and wonder why on earth she wasn't just going for it. The man affected her in a way she wasn't used to. Certainly, in a way that Rafa didn't, and perhaps no man ever had.

"Would you rather I leave?"

Her heart stopped beating at that. Of all the things she might have expected him to say, that was not one of them. She met his gaze. He raised one eyebrow as he looked earnestly back at her.

"I thought perhaps, now that our friends are beginning their new life together, you and I should get to know each other better."

She wasn't sure if his fingers caressed her thigh as he said that or if it was her imagination as she thought about the ways that they might get to know each other better.

"But if you prefer, I will leave."

She held his gaze. It was a challenge, and she knew it. He was giving her the option to back out. But she didn't want to. She should want to. This was a bad, bad idea. But if she told him to go, he'd have won.

She shook her head slowly. "I'm not afraid of you. And I'm not going to fall for any of the moves you put on me. But I do agree that we should probably find a way to get along—for Audrey and Ted's sake."

There was no mistaking the way his hand moved a little farther up her thigh—or the way she reacted to it before he sat back with a smile. "Thank you."

The waiter returned with their drinks, and Izzy took hers gratefully. She was going to need one to survive this guy!

~ ~ ~

Diego raised his glass to her. "Can we call a truce?" His heart was pounding in his chest. He'd only rested his hand on her leg to see how she'd react. He'd expected another brush off. What he hadn't expected was the way she'd closed her eyes or the rush that he had felt. He'd flown too close to the sun, and he had no desire to fall.

She pursed her lips and took a sip of her drink. "I think we should. If your intention is for us to become friends so that we can be supportive of Ted and Audrey, then I think you should drop the whole act."

He raised an eyebrow. "Act?"

She chuckled. "Come on, Diego. The whole ..." she shrugged. "Sexy guy, charmer thing you have going."

He tried to bite back a laugh but didn't quite succeed. "Sexy guy, charmer?"

She rolled her eyes. "Yes. You know damned well what I mean. You pull it every time I'm around you. To be fair, I'm sure you do it around every woman you ever meet. In fact, that gives me an idea. If we're going to be friends, then you should probably not think of me as a woman at all."

He shook his head slowly. "Impossible."

She let out a short laugh. "Drop it, would you?"

"It's not an act, Isobel. It's true." He let his gaze travel over her, taking in her short, blonde hair, her beautiful face, the breasts that always drew his eyes and the body that had haunted his mind far too often since he'd met her. How could she ever expect of him to think of her as anything but a woman—and a very beautiful woman at that.

"See!" She exclaimed. "That is exactly what I'm talking about. You expect me to be turned on by that, don't you?"

He looked up into her eyes and smiled. "You aren't?"

She pursed her lips. "I'm not a liar. You're a good-looking man, Diego. When your eyes make suggestions like that, a woman is going to respond."

He couldn't help but smile. He knew the effect that look had on women, but until she admitted it, he hadn't been sure of the effect it had on her. "What is your response?"

She laughed. "You don't give up, do you? In fact, don't bother to answer that. If you want to call a truce with all the flirting and come-ons, then yes, I think it would come in handy—for our sake as well as Audrey and Ted's—for us to be friends. It'll make life easier. But if you're going to keep up with the sex hound act, then I'm out."

"Sex hound?"

She laughed again. "You know what I mean. I can't think of the right word for it."

"I do. Forgive me?"

She nodded, and he couldn't help but smile as he raised her hand to his lips and kissed the back of it.

She gave him a dark look, and he let her go. "You need to understand. It's not an act. It's who I am."

~ ~ ~

Izzy gave him a puzzled look. "I believe that. You're just one of those guys who pursues every woman he meets and—"

"Only the most beautiful ones," he interrupted.

She pursed her lips. "Okay. Even if I roll with that. You pursue every beautiful woman who crosses your path, in the hopes of sleeping with her, right? Like I said, you're a sex hound." The name brought that smirk to his lips again, but she couldn't think of a better way to put it. "So, what I want to know is what you're doing here?"

"I came to see you."

"But you already know that I'm not going to sleep with you."

He shrugged. For the first time, he looked serious. There was no smirk, no laughter in his eyes.

"So, why are you here?"

To her surprise, he put his arm around her shoulders and leaned closer. "Do you want to know the truth?"

Her heart was racing. She wasn't sure if it was the nearness of him or eager anticipation of what he was about to say. She looked up into his eyes, and he chuckled.

"The truth is, I have no idea!" He wasn't teasing. He shook his head slowly as though he was baffled by the question. "I wish I could tell you why I flew here with Ted when I have no plans to go to the lake this weekend. I wish I could tell you why I was so eager to see you when I know you don't want to see me. I wish I could answer your question. I really do."

"You only came to see me?"

He nodded.

She felt as though fireworks were exploding in her chest. "And you didn't just come because you thought we might get to spend the afternoon in bed together?"

He held her gaze for a moment. "I know that that is not an option." He looked as serious as she'd ever seen him. "You made it very clear the last time I was here. You have your young man."

Izzy felt bad about that. She'd only used Rafa as an excuse. She'd claimed he was the reason that she couldn't sleep with Diego, but they'd never been a real couple—never even been exclusive. She'd only seen him twice since Diego had been here and she hadn't slept with him. Her heart thudded to a halt as she realized that the reason Rafa had lost his appeal for her was because he wasn't Diego.

He was watching her face now. "You do still have your young man?"

Her heart restarted and was back to pounding again. If she told him that Rafa was out of the picture, then …? No. "Even if …"

Diego's smile was back. "You're not seeing him anymore? You are single?"

She pursed her lips. She hated the way that sounded. It made her feel like an old maid. "What does it matter?" she asked. "I'm sure you're not single."

He looked thoughtful, and she wondered if he was about to admit that he did indeed have a girlfriend or three. "Do you want to know the truth?"

"I tend to prefer it over lies."

He chuckled. "Very well. Then I shall tell you a shocking fact about my love life."

Izzy wasn't sure she wanted to hear this.

He tightened his arm around her shoulders, and the twinkle was back in his eye when he spoke again. "This is a fact that I wasn't even aware of myself until this morning. It took Ted to point it out to me." He nodded to himself before he continued.

"Go on then, spit it out. What kind of shock am I in for?"

He smiled. "I have not been on a date—been with a woman since the day I met you."

Wow! What was he getting at? She laughed. "Do you mean to say that I've put you off women?"

He didn't join her laughter. "It would appear that you have. At least, you've put me off every woman who isn't you." He held her gaze.

She didn't know what to say. Part of her wanted to believe that he was still teasing her, but there was something serious in his eyes.

"And what do you expect me to do about that?"

He shrugged. "I didn't expect you to do a thing. I came with Ted because I wanted to see you—to see if you still have the same effect on me. You do. However, I knew—at least, I thought I knew that you were seeing your young trainer. Now, I know that you aren't."

She hadn't exactly told him that she wasn't seeing Rafa anymore, but she hadn't denied that she was single either.

She looked up into his big, brown eyes and smiled. When he smiled back, all the teasing and pretense were gone, and if it were possible, he was even more handsome.

"And what do you want me to do now?" she asked.

"Kiss me." As he said it, his hand came up to cup her cheek. Shivers chased each other down her spine as his fingers slid into her hair, and he drew her closer. He looked down at her lips and then back up into her eyes. He really was irresistible. His lips were full and soft as they brushed over hers. His arm around her shoulders held her closer to him, and she felt as though he surrounded her. As he claimed her mouth in a kiss that stole her senses, she felt as though she was drowning in a sea of Diego—and she didn't want to come up for air.

~ ~ ~

When he lifted his head, Diego's heart was racing. He'd daydreamed about kissing this woman, but even that hadn't been as good as the reality. She looked dazed. She felt it, too; he knew she did.

"Wow!" She let out a little laugh. "I wasn't expecting that."

"I wasn't either."

She looked skeptical. "You weren't? Isn't that what you came here for?"

"I told you. I thought you were still seeing your young trainer. I would never kiss another man's woman."

Her eyes flashed at that. "I'm my own woman."

"Forgive me. It's a turn of phrase; that is all."

She pursed her lips. "I'll forgive you if you promise to understand that I am my own woman. I'm not and never will be some man's property."

"I give you my word."

She relaxed and smiled at him. "So, what's your next move?"

He chuckled. "I need to have a move?"

"I'm sure you do."

He didn't have any moves planned. She'd taken him by surprise. He'd expected that his visit this afternoon would be short and not very sweet—that he'd probably be back at the airport within the hour waiting for Karl to return from the lake to take him home with his tail between his legs.

He wasn't about to let this fortunate turn of events throw him off, though. He was better than that. He sat back in his seat and curled his foot around her ankle.

"Well, I don't mind telling you that you've surprised me. I truly didn't come here with any moves in mind. But …" He stroked her calf with his foot. "If you're interested, I have an empty weekend stretching ahead of me. Would you like to share it?"

He held his breath. He wasn't sure where that suggestion had even come from. But now that it was out there, he hoped that she would agree.

She cocked her head to one side. "The weekend?"

He nodded.

She shook her head in wonder. "I expected you to suggest we go back to my place. You know, occupy your time until the plane can get back here to pick you up."

He waggled his eyebrows. "We can do that first if you like."

She laughed, but he got the impression that she wouldn't be against the idea. "And what are you suggesting we would do with this empty weekend that you're looking to fill?"

"I'd like to invite you to my home." He had to think fast here. Of course, he wanted to sleep with her, but he was past the age when he'd have been able to keep her busy in bed for a whole weekend. "We can hang out. Walk the beach, browse downtown Laguna, have you ever been?"

"Not for years."

He couldn't resist smiling as he remembered several of the conversations they'd had. "Say you want to come with me?"

She met his gaze. She understood what he was asking. She nodded slowly. "Okay."

# Chapter Eight

Izzy's hands shook as she turned the key in the front door. It'd been a couple of months since the last time Diego was here, but he still had the same effect on her. On the drive back to her place, she'd kept wondering why she was doing this. This was a bad idea. Or was it? What was wrong with it? Diego was a nice guy. He was sexy as sin. She wanted him; she wasn't going to deny that, so what was wrong with bringing him home? She swallowed ... what was wrong with spending the weekend with him?

He was going to be a part of her life in some capacity because of Audrey and Ted. She turned the handle, and the door swung open. Perhaps it was better to get the sexual attraction out of their systems now. Then, over time, they could hopefully become friends.

He followed her into the hallway and waited while she closed the door. It felt as though he filled the whole space. There was no way around him, no way past him. He stepped toward her, and she looked up into his eyes. The heat of the look he gave her sent ripples of desire coursing through her. What the hell? He was possibly the most handsome man she'd ever known.

He wanted her; he'd made that clear. Why shouldn't she just relax and enjoy this … enjoy his company … enjoy him?

His arms came around her waist, and she reached hers up around his neck. Shockwaves raced through her as he pressed her up against the wall. The feel of his hard body against hers made her knees go weak. His hand came up to cup her cheek, but instead of moving in for the kiss as she expected, he smiled at her.

"You're beautiful, Isobel."

She searched his face. She wanted to believe it was a line, but he sure looked like he meant it. He felt like he meant it. There was an intensity in his eyes that she didn't know what to do with. She chuckled. "I'm sure you don't need me to tell you, but you're not so bad yourself."

His eyebrows came down. Jeez! Was his ego that big that he couldn't take a joke? He must know just how gorgeous he was. Women probably told him all the time—right before they gave in to his charms.

He looked down at her lips, and she couldn't wait. They didn't need to get caught up in conversation or even go through the motions of saying the right things. They were going to do this, so they might as well get on with it.

She closed the gap between their lips and reached up to sink her fingers in his hair. Damn, the man could kiss. He started out slowly, tenderly, and built up until he'd claimed her mouth. His tongue was exploring her—as were his hands—and she was melting against him.

His hands came down to hold her hips, and he pressed himself against her. She moaned into his mouth at the feel of him. Wow! He was a big boy. He ground his hips against hers, and she moved with him, overtaken by the sensations that rolled through her. She clung to his shoulders, wondering in amazement whether he was about to take her over the edge—

right here in the hallway while they were both still fully clothed.

She let out another little moan, this time in disappointment, when he lifted his head and stepped away from her. He leaned back against the opposite wall. "Forgive me?"

She laughed. "What for? For stopping? I'm not sure I can."

A smile touched his lips. "No?"

"No."

"I didn't want to … We should take our time."

"Oh, no. You're not pulling that one on me again. She took hold of his hand and started leading him toward the stairs.

"Pulling what?"

She couldn't believe she was going to say it, but she did. "What you did to me at the lodge that first weekend. When you walked me back to my room. You deliberately got me warmed up and then walked away and left me wanting you."

That might be the biggest smile she'd seen on his face yet. "You wanted me?"

She laughed. "You know damned well I did."

They'd reached her bedroom, and she pulled him inside. She started to unbutton her blouse, but he came to her and took hold of her hands. "May I?"

She looked up at him. One eyebrow was raised in question. She couldn't for the life of her figure him out. She'd have expected him to be stripping his own clothes off, eager to get down to it, not to be wanting to take the time to undress her.

She sucked in a deep breath as he unfastened her top button. He smiled and dropped a kiss on her lips. "You know how much I've admired these girls from afar."

She chuckled, but it came out sounding a little strangled. "It's hard to miss. You talk to them more than you talk to me."

He gave her a shamefaced smile and continued unfastening buttons. "They usually seem more pleased to see me than you do."

She bit her bottom lips as she looked down. Her nipples stood erect, confirming his words.

It was a huge turn on to watch his big hands slowly work their way down to the bottom until her blouse fell open. He rested his hands on her ribcage; his skin looked so dark against hers. This was torture. She hadn't expected him to want to take his time like this, it was driving her crazy with desire for him.

His thumbs stroked her through her bra, making her close her eyes and let her head fall back. When her bra was gone, he closed his hands around her, and they both let out a sigh.

She realized that if they were undressing each other, then she was falling behind. She reached for his belt, but he shifted away from her. "All in good time, Miss Isobel."

He was still caressing her breasts, and her mind was too fuzzy to argue. He lowered his head, and she sank her fingers in his hair when he mouthed her nipple. That felt so good!

He walked her back to the bed until her legs hit it, and she sat down. He wasted no time getting rid of her pants, and then she was sitting there in just her panties, and he was fully dressed. She wanted to see him, to touch him. She reached for his belt again, but he smiled and moved away. "Patience."

He knelt down between her legs—at eye level with her breasts. She clung to his shoulders as he licked and sucked, tormenting her with his talented tongue. She gasped when his hand slid inside her panties. He stroked her entrance and dipped a finger inside her, making her cling tighter to him.

"I'm ready," she breathed.

He lifted his head and gave her a puzzled look. She was hardly going to spell it out for him that yes, he'd done his job, she was wet, and it would be okay now.

"So am I." He smiled.

Phew! Finally, she was going to see him and see just what she was in for. The feel of his arousal when he'd pressed it against her had her eager if a little apprehensive.

Instead of undressing as she'd expected him to, he put a hand to her shoulder and laid her back on the bed. Then his fingers were inside her panties again, this time pulling them to the side, and ... oh! ... His mouth was on her. She grabbed fistfuls of sheet underneath her, and her back arched up as he proved just how talented his tongue really was.

He rested two fingers at her entrance, tormenting her with anticipation. She could feel herself getting closer, and apparently, he could, too. His mouth closed around her, and his fingers slid deep, thrusting in and out and taking her over the edge. Her back arched up off the bed as she let herself go. "Yes!"

When she lay still, he came up to join her, lying behind her and closing his arms around her. Wow! She'd expected him to be getting his pants off ready for his turn.

He nuzzled his lips into her neck. "Was it good?"

She nodded. "Very, very good."

She could feel him smile. "Good. I want to please you."

"You did." She rolled over to face him. "Want me to return the favor?"

He frowned.

Maybe he didn't understand what she meant? She could hardly believe that. She reached for his buckle, and this time he didn't stop her. She pushed his pants down and slid her hand inside his shorts, then bit her lip. Damn! He was a big boy.

He met her gaze and smiled. She smiled back and started to move down over him. He caught her arm and pulled her back up. "Let's take our time?"

"Seriously?" She'd didn't think she'd ever known a guy to turn down a blow job.

He nodded. "Seriously. I want us to get to know each other. He ran his hand over her shoulder and down the back of her arm, and for some reason, that felt strangely intimate. He closed his arm around her and held her close to his chest, making her close her eyes and sigh. It felt so good—and they weren't even doing anything!

She needed to remedy that. She unbuttoned his shirt and pushed it back off his shoulders; he got rid of his pants and shorts. Once he lay naked, she let her gaze travel over him. He'd done that to her so often, she kind of wanted him to know how it felt. It had the opposite effect, though. She discovered how it must make him feel. It turned her on so much to take in every detail of his big, muscled body. His broad shoulders, the dusting of dark and silver hair on his chest. The V shape that led down to ... she swallowed—to that thing!

She looked up at him. "Is that why you're so full of yourself?"

He laughed out loud. "Perhaps it is. I hadn't thought of it that way before, but you may well be right."

He took her hand and placed it over him. He let out a slow breath as she curled her fingers around him.

She wanted to come out with some joke, something to make them laugh and break the moment, but her brain couldn't do it. She was under his spell but then looking at his face, it seemed that he was under hers, too.

She stroked the length of him, up and down, enjoying the look on his face as he surrendered to her. She couldn't wait. She put a hand to his shoulder and turned him onto his back and then straddled him.

He raised an eyebrow. "You like to be in charge?"

She nodded, hoping that wouldn't be an issue right now. She knew he likely wanted to be the big man, putting it to the little woman on his terms, but she couldn't do that. She stroked herself with the tip of him, hoping to distract him before he rolled her off.

It worked. He closed his eyes and moved his hips in time with her. He closed his hands around her waist when she guided him toward her, and she braced herself for the moment when he would pull her down onto him.

He didn't.

He only rocked his hips gently as she slowly lowered herself onto him in her own time. Damn! He felt good. He was so big.

He met her gaze, and she closed her eyes and started to move.

When she opened them again, he was still looking and this time, her eyes locked with his and she couldn't look away. Their bodies moved together, faster and faster. He let her move the way she needed to. His hands still held her hips, but it felt like he was supporting her, not clamping her where he wanted her to receive him.

The tension was building inside her. Every thrust of his hips took her closer to the edge. She sat up and wanted to let her head fall back, but she still couldn't tear her eyes away from his. She was gasping now as he drove her to the point of no return.

"Oh!" She gasped as all the tension inside her found its release, and her orgasm tore through her. She felt him tense, and then he joined her, feeling as though he was filling her and the whole universe around them with exploding stars. "Yes. Yes. Yes!"

When she finally slumped down on his chest, he closed his arms around her. One hand came up to tangle in her hair. She lifted her head and looked down into his eyes. She'd have expected him to be the kind to roll her off and head straight for the bathroom. Not to hold her like this.

He gave her a lazy smile and ran his hand down over her ass. "Now, we're starting to get to know each other."

She just stared at him. She had no idea what to say. She'd half expected that this would be the end of getting to know each other—that once he'd gotten what he'd come for, the offer of a weekend in Laguna would disappear.

He raised an eyebrow. "I know I pleased you ... it's not that, so what is it?"

She had to laugh. "Your ego! You just know that you pleased me?"

He smirked. "Of course, I felt, I saw, I heard how much."

She rolled off him, not wanting to tell him what she'd been thinking. He surprised her again when he turned to lie face to face with her and planted a kiss on her lips. "And just so there's no doubt, you pleased me, too."

She wanted to come back with some sassy remark, but the look on his face stopped her. He was pleased with himself, sure. But he wasn't being cocky or arrogant. He was happy that he'd pleased her as he put it, and he wanted her to be happy that she'd pleased him, too. What was wrong with that? Nothing, if she stopped thinking of him as just a guy who was just looking to get laid. But if she stopped thinking of him that way, then she didn't know what the hell to think.

Diego took hold of her hand as the plane thundered down the runway. When he'd decided to fly over here with Ted this afternoon, he hadn't known how things would go. He'd believed that Izzy would most likely turn him away. He'd wanted to see her again, to test Ted's theory that he was, in fact, hung up on her. But he'd been under no illusions that she

might be hung up on him. The fact that she was no longer
seeing her trainer had been a very pleasant surprise. That she'd
agreed to come with him this weekend had surprised him even
more.

He wasn't surprised how good they were in bed together,
though. He'd known since the first time he met her that if they
ever went there, it would be amazing. And it had been.

"How long will it take us to get there?"

"Only around twenty minutes."

"Wow!" She shook her head. "It'd take more than two hours
on the road—especially on a Friday like this."

He nodded. "Ted and I are fortunate that we can do this."

She held his gaze for a long moment, and he got the
impression that she wanted to know how he'd gotten so
fortunate. He waited for the question, but it didn't come. She
turned to look out of the window again.

"Would you like to go out to dinner, or would you rather eat
at my place?"

She turned back. "You cook?"

He laughed. "Why so skeptical all the time, Miss Isobel? I'm
a very good cook."

"You know that now you've said that I have to put your
claim to the test, don't you?"

He chuckled. "I should have known. Then tonight we eat at
home; I'll cook for you. And tomorrow, we can go out."

Her smile faded.

"What is it?"

"You really want to spend the whole weekend together?"

"Of course, I do. I asked. You said yes. You packed a bag.
You don't want to?" He was finding it hard to understand her.
She'd been wary of him at first. Dismissive of him, but he'd
put that down to the fact that she wasn't interested because
she was seeing a younger man. Now, there was no younger

man in the picture, and she'd proved that she was interested in him—physically, at least. But she kept blowing hot and cold— or perhaps simply still assuming that his only interest in her was physical.

She blew out a sigh. "I'm sorry. I do." She met his gaze, and for the first time, he felt as though she was being completely honest with him. "I think I need to relax and accept that you're not the guy I thought you were."

"Who did you think I was?"

She gave him a wry smile. "A sex hound."

He laughed. "I won't deny that I find you sexy—or that I'm hoping to spend at least some of the weekend in bed with you, but no, I am not a sex hound."

"Okay. Well, since we've gotten that out of the way. What's the deal here?"

He raised an eyebrow, not understanding.

"What are we doing if we're not just sleeping together?"

"We're getting to know each other."

"You mean you want to be friends because of Audrey and Ted?" She smiled. "Friends with occasional benefits?"

He shook his head slowly. "I want to get to know you, Izzy. In your own right, for your own sake—and mine. We took a back seat to them. But that's because they're our friends, and we look out for them. They're not like us, and we both wanted to make sure that they got the chance to get to know each other and to see where things could go between them. Now, they know; they've begun their journey together." He held her gaze for a moment before he added. "I'd like to see where ours might go."

Her eyes widened as she looked back at him. She didn't say anything for a long time, and Diego almost regretted having spoken so frankly. Almost, but she needed to understand his intentions—now that he knew what they were. And he needed to know if that wasn't going to work for her.

"You think we have a journey of our own to go on?" She looked shocked—and not in a good way.

"I'd like to. Wouldn't you?"

She frowned. "I don't know, Diego. I mean, you're a good guy. Better than I was giving you credit for, but …"

His heart was hammering in his chest as he waited for her to continue. Over the course of this afternoon—ever since Ted's revelation this morning that he hadn't shown any interest in another woman since he'd met her—he'd realized that he was interested in exploring what could happen between them.

"But what?" he asked when he couldn't wait any longer.

She shrugged. "I didn't see it coming. And to be honest, you're the kind of guy I normally avoid."

He'd known that. He had so much going against him in her eyes—his age being the biggest obstacle. He smiled, hoping to get her smiling back. "You're telling me that you don't like handsome, you don't like well-endowed, and you don't like successful?"

She rolled her eyes and let out a short laugh. "It's the ego that goes with them that I don't know how to handle."

He pursed his lips. "I think you can. I think you like it if you're honest with yourself. I cannot make myself into some mealy-mouthed little yes-man who you can push around. You're a strong woman, Izzy. You might enjoy pushing little boys around in bed, but what you need is a strong man beside you."

Her first reaction was anger, he could see it flash across her face, but to her credit, she let it go and considered what he'd said. "It's not that I like men I can push around; it's just that I can't stand men who want to push me around."

"I would never do that." It surprised him that she saw him that way. He took hold of her hand and brought it to his lips. "Never."

She nodded slowly. "I believe you. But I'm playing catch up here. I told you you're not what I thought, but I'm not sure where that leaves me."

"So, take your time to work it out. We have the weekend ahead of us. Perhaps by the time I bring you home, you'll have a better idea of who I am—and what you want to do with me."

"Okay. That's fair. Let's just have a fun weekend and see what happens, why don't we?"

# Chapter Nine

Izzy leaned on the steel rail and stared out at the ocean. The metal felt cool beneath her skin. It felt real—and she could use a good dose of reality right about now. She felt as though she'd somehow stepped into some romantic movie—only no one had told the director that she was the wrong actress for the role.

She wasn't the kind of girl to be bowled over by Diego's big beautiful house. Not the kind who would fall for the tall, good-looking hero and look on adoringly as he saved the world. She was her own person—not a supporting actress in someone else's life. Not even if the someone else was a wealthy, successful, gorgeous man, who appeared to be interested in her and who, much to her surprise, was turning out to be a genuinely decent person.

She took a sip of her drink and blew out a sigh. But if she wanted to put all that aside, she could just relax and enjoy the weekend with him.

He came back out and leaned on the rail beside her. He tucked a strand of hair behind her ear, and the way her body reacted to him did indeed make her want to enjoy the weekend with him.

"Are you all right?"

She smiled. "I am. How could I not be? I'm in this beautiful place, with a very nice man, who just happens to be cooking dinner for me."

"But you're not sure you want to be here."

She turned and met his gaze. "What makes you say that?"

"When I came back out, you were looking out at the ocean with a faraway look in your eyes. As if there's somewhere else you'd like to be."

"No. There isn't. I'm glad I'm here." She looked around. "This place is wonderful." She tapped a finger in the middle of his chest. "I'll even admit; you are wonderful."

He smiled at that. "But what?"

"But I don't feel like I fit in."

"What do you mean?"

"You, this place, all of this. You need some young blonde barbie to complete the picture. Not someone like me. You need someone who'll hang on your every word and admire everything you do."

He let out a short laugh. "You think I'm that superficial?"

"No! Sorry. I didn't mean that in a bad way. It's just that's what completes the picture, isn't it?"

"Not my picture, no. I don't need a woman to bolster my ego." He winked at her. "You already know that it's robust enough. I know some men feel that being with a younger woman proves their ... their ..." He frowned as he searched for the word and then smiled when he found it. "Their virility."

She nodded. He might say *some* men, but she believed it was all of them.

He moved behind her and rested his hands on the railing on either side of hers. Shivers ran through her when he spoke next to her ear and pressed himself against her. "I've never doubted my own virility." The feel of him pressing against her ass made clear why he wouldn't need to question!

"But, Izzy, it makes me sad that you feel that way. What can I do? How can I convince you that that's not who I am?"

He straightened up and slid his arm around her waist, pulling her back against him. She relaxed and leaned back as he nibbled at her neck. "If I thought you were some weak and willing little lady, do you think I would have asked you here? Forgive me, but I wouldn't have needed to fly to Ventura for that. Women like that are everywhere. Women like you don't come along every day—I want to say that women like you only come along once in a lifetime."

She spun around to look at him. There he went spouting crap again! He was so full of it. She froze when she saw the look in his eyes. He wasn't feeding her lines—he was serious!

"What? What did I do wrong?"

She shook her head. "You mean that, don't you?"

He nodded solemnly and closed his arms around her again. "I do. I feel so lucky that you're here. I want to show you who I am." He smiled. "I want you to like what you see and fall for me. I want to get to know you and fall for you. But I know that first I must earn your respect and your affection."

His eyes were serious as they looked down into hers. They dropped down to look at her lips, and she knew what was coming. He cupped her cheek and then his lips came down on hers and she was lost.

His kisses were intoxicating. She loved the way he made her feel with big arms closed around her and that big ... pressing into her belly. In her experience, a kiss like that was simply a precursor. It was the first warmup before sex. But when Diego lifted his head, he hugged her closer and dropped a kiss on top of her head.

"The things you do to me, Miss Isobel."

She tightened her arms around his waist and allowed herself to relax and rest her cheek against his chest. She had to ask herself just what it was he was doing to her.

Diego smiled to himself when he felt her relax. It seemed she had a low opinion of men in general, and him, in particular. He could only guess that perhaps he reminded her of someone who had not treated her well.

Her suspicion of him and his motives only made him want to show her just how wrong she was. Of course, he liked sex. He'd been honest with her that he had many female friends who looked forward to his call for just that reason. But that wasn't all he was about. And there was something about her, something that made him want to step up and be about so much more than sex.

He had always believed that a man and a woman could come together and make each other better. He believed that great couples were made up of two strong and independent people who didn't need each other for anything, but who wanted each other. He believed all of that was possible, but he'd never met a woman who made him want to try it. Not until Izzy. She was strong and she was smart; she was proud, and she was so, so sexy. He held her a little closer still as he roused at the memory of her bouncing above him this afternoon.

He dropped another kiss on top of her head and let her go. He had to, or he'd be taking her to his bedroom for more. He wanted more, but he planned to save it for later. First, he'd promised her dinner.

He took her hand and led her back inside the house.

She looked around her as they went. "This place is something else."

He raised an eyebrow at her. "Is that a good thing?"

She laughed. "Err, yeah! It's amazing. I would have had you down for a Mediterranean style place, not all this modern steel and glass."

It was his turn to laugh at that. "When we go to Ted's place, you'll see that he's the one with the Mediterranean style. I prefer sleek and modern."

"So, I see." A small frown furrowed her brow, and he'd guess that she was questioning why the two of them would go to Ted's. She wasn't yet seeing the possibility of them as a couple in the same way that he was. He smiled to himself. That was okay; she would. And in the meantime, he'd just keep dropping little hints like that to get her used to the idea.

"Would you like to eat in the dining room or right here?" He'd started to set two places at the dining table earlier but then thought better of it. It was a wonderful place for dinner parties, but for just the two of them, it might feel too formal— and he didn't want her to get the idea that he was trying to impress her or win her over with what he had instead of who he was.

He'd been right. She pulled out one of the barstools at the island. "I think right here would be great."

He poured two glasses of wine and brought one to her. She took it with a smile. "Thank you. And I have to tell you, dinner smells delicious."

"It will be." He served up two plates and came to sit beside her. He watched as she took a bite and had to close his eyes when she moaned. He knew that sound.

"Oh, my God! That's wonderful."

"I told you I can cook."

She laughed. "You can! You can cook for me anytime."

He met her gaze and smiled. "I'd love to."

Her smile faded, and she looked into his eyes. All her cynicism and sass were gone. It wasn't fear in her eyes. He understood now that she wasn't afraid of him. But there was something, some hesitation. Up until now, it had been easy to see that she just didn't buy almost anything he said. Now, he'd guess that she was buying it, but she wasn't sure if she wanted to believe it. He knew he wouldn't win her over with words. He'd have to prove to her over time that he was serious about exploring what might happen between them.

"I make wonderful eggs benedict if you want that for breakfast."

She nodded.

It was probably too soon, but he decided to go for it. "And if you want, when I take you home, I'll stick around and be your personal chef."

She laughed. "As if!"

He should have known she'd think he was joking. "I will. I don't have to go into the office anymore. I can shop and cook for you while you're at work and have dinner waiting on the table for you when you get home." He said it because he got the impression that part of what she distrusted in him was the fact that she saw him as such a macho man. She'd made comments to that effect whenever they'd been up at the lake.

To his surprise, she didn't play along or even turn him down flat. Instead, she looked sad. "You'd only be under my feet if you were to cook while I'm working. I don't get to go to the office anymore, either, remember?"

Of course. How could he have forgotten? She and Audrey had given up their office. She was going to work remotely now. From the look on her face, she wasn't thrilled about that. "Sorry. I do." He smiled. "I can cook quietly?"

"That's okay. I don't think you'd cope in my kitchen anyway. Not when you're used to this."

She might have a point there. Her house was nice, but her kitchen was small. Not big enough for him to make his mess anyway. He wasn't going to go down that road, though. No way was he about to start comparing her house and his. He got the impression that it was just one more thing that she might hold against him. He smiled as a ridiculous thought struck him. He should probably wait, but he wanted to ... He opened his mouth and then thought better of it. He should wait until Sunday. Perhaps by then, she might even consider the crazy idea. Right now, she wouldn't even believe he was serious.

"Just know that the offer stands. I will be happy to cook for you any time you want me to."

"Thank you. That's sweet of you." She watched his face as if she expected him to react in some way.

He smiled. "What can I say? You bring out my sweet side, Miss Isobel."

~ ~ ~

Diego pulled the car into a spot and cut the engine. "Do you want to walk or drink or dance?"

"Maybe walk?" It was a beautiful evening, and Izzy remembered there being a path that followed the coastline.

"Beach or downtown? Do you want to see the stores or the ocean?"

"The ocean. We're coming to see the stores tomorrow, right?"

He nodded. "Your wish is my command."

He sure made her feel that that was the case. He'd made her a wonderful dinner and asked what she wanted to do next. Sitting out on his terrace with him, the way he looked in the last glow of evening sunlight, what she'd really wanted to do was take him to bed. But since he was making such a big effort to show her that this weekend was about more than that, she'd asked him to bring her into town. They'd be going to bed later anyway.

She watched the lights flash on the car as he locked it. She was fairly certain that the car was worth as much as her house. She'd known he was loaded, but the reality of just how much—his house, his car, the plane—was a lot to take in. She pulled herself together. She shouldn't hold it against him.

He came around the car and took hold of her hand. "You look sad again."

She gave him a bright smile. "Sad? What on earth would I be sad about?" She was slipping. Normally, when she went out with a guy, she made sure that she was bright and upbeat, keep them laughing, and they were happy. More importantly, it kept them at bay. When they were entertained, they didn't have the time or the interest to ask questions, to find out who she really was, and that was for the best.

Diego was proving to be a different breed than the guys she usually dated. And not just because he was twenty years older.

"I wish you'd tell me." His big brown eyes were concerned as he raised an eyebrow at her. "I have seen you as the bubbly, outgoing one, and yet, I feel there's so much more going on with you. You don't want to share it with me?"

She held his gaze for a moment. There was nothing to share, was there? She was doing a little reflecting; that was all. Though why this big beautiful man was making her think so much, she didn't know.

She surprised him by reaching up and planting a kiss on his lips. "I am sharing with you. I shared my bed this afternoon. We'll share yours later. I'm sharing the whole weekend with you." She tugged his hand and started toward the crosswalk.

Once they were on the path that followed the beach and then led up the hill, he slung his arm around her shoulders. It just showed how little he knew about her. Rafa knew better than to try that. She didn't like to be crowded. She glanced up at Diego. Strangely enough, she didn't feel that way with him.

Even though he was so much bigger than Rafa, she didn't feel as though he was invading her space—more like he was sharing it.

"What are you going to do with yourself now you don't have to go into the office every day?" she asked. She could imagine him being one of those guys who came down into town and hung out on the terraces outside the bars and cafes—watching the world and the women go by.

"I'll probably still go in whenever I'm here. I wouldn't know what to do with myself otherwise. But I don't plan to be here very much. I'm hoping to close on the house at the lake soon."

"Oh, of course." The last time she'd seen him, he'd found a house that he wanted to buy in Summer Lake. "And what will you do up there?"

He smiled. "Spend time with my son and his fiancée." He looked happy about that. And even happier when he added. "They're getting married soon, and when they do, they want to start a family." His smile grew even bigger. "I'm going to be a grandpa."

Izzy forced herself to smile. She was happy for him, she really was. Of course, she envied him, but he didn't need to know that.

"And what about you? How much will things change for you now Audrey's gone?"

She made a face. "I'm happy for her, I really am."

His arm tightened around her shoulders, and she got the feeling that he understood what she wasn't saying; she was happy for Audrey but sad for herself.

"I need to figure out some new routines. I'm used to going into the office all week, hanging out with Audrey and her kids on the weekends. Other than that, I go to the gym …" She faltered when she saw his expression change.

"Just to be clear. You're not seeing your trainer anymore?"

Part of her wanted to tell him it was none of his business. She saw who she wanted when she wanted, and it was up to her to decide what she wanted—not up to him to respect some other guy's property rights. But that was just her own shit getting in the way. He was trying to be a decent guy, and she didn't need to bite his head off for it. "I'm not."

"Do you mind if I ask why?"

She looked up at him, wondering why he wanted to know.

He raised an eyebrow and waited.

She shrugged. "It was never anything serious."

"And now it's over?"

She nodded.

"Good."

"Why?"

He stopped walking and slid his arms around her waist, forcing her to look up to see his face. "I thought that would be obvious by now."

"Well, it isn't."

"I'm glad that you're not seeing him anymore because I want to start seeing you."

She held his gaze for a long moment. He'd kept hinting all afternoon that that was where he was going, but she found it hard to believe. Surely this weekend was just a time for them to hang out, have sex, and then each go on their way. Of course, they'd run into each other again, because of Audrey and Ted, but she doubted it would happen too often. "Why?"

"You want me to spell it out for you?"

She nodded. The way he asked made it seem as though his reasons should be perfectly obvious—but they weren't to her.

"Because I find you irresistible, Miss Isobel. I can't get you out of my mind. I've already told you that I have not seen another woman since the day we met." He smiled. "You are fully aware that I like women. I like their company, and I like sex. And since you have put me off all other women, you are the only one left. I want to enjoy your company." He winked and added, "And have sex."

"Are you sure this isn't some game you play with all your women?" She found it hard to accept that there was any possibility that he was serious.

His eyebrows came down and knit together. "Why won't you believe me? What can I do?"

She shrugged. "Don't get mad!"

"I'm not mad, Izzy. I'm frustrated. I'm bowled over by you. I want us to spend time together and have fun. But I can't even get past the first hurdle of making you believe that I mean it."

His hands came up to the cup the sides of her neck, and her eyelids drooped as he claimed her mouth in one of those amazing kisses.

When he lifted his head, he looked down into her eyes. "Does that not tell you anything?"

She smiled. "It tells me that you're a good kisser."

He pursed his lips.

"It tells me that you like me."

The hint of a smile played on his lips. "What else?"

"It tells me that I probably don't want to be out here, walking for hours."

"And why's that?"

"Because I think I'd rather you take me home again and make good on what that kiss just promised."

He narrowed his eyes at her. But she didn't know how to go anywhere near the conversation that he wanted to have. It was easier to distract him with more sex—and besides, it was true. Every time he kissed her, it felt as though he was promising her more good things to come.

He blew out a short sigh. "Do you want to at least walk a little way?"

She gave him a sassy smile. "Sure. Why don't we walk as far as your car? Then we can take it home—to bed."

# Chapter Ten

Diego opened his eyes, surprised to see the sun shining brightly through the windows. It was late, at least much later than he usually woke up. He smiled when he remembered why. Izzy.

He turned his head, and there she was. Her face was relaxed in sleep. He wasn't surprised that they'd slept late—they'd worn each other out last night. He reached out to draw her closer to him. He loved the feel of her in his arms. He didn't want to question that too much. Waking up beside a woman wasn't unusual. Though, it was more usual that he would be in her bed rather than his. And in the morning, he liked to keep his distance as best he could. Women seemed to believe that the morning after was for bonding, whereas he felt that it was for saying thank you … and goodbye.

Her eyes fluttered as he held her to his chest, but she didn't open them. He pressed a kiss into her hair and smiled to himself as she mumbled something. If she wasn't ready to wake up, he'd let her sleep on. He shifted his hips away from her. That part of him was fully awake, but it could wait. She seemed to have no problem getting close to him in that way, but holding her like this was a pleasure she denied him more often than not when she was awake.

He breathed in the scent of her. She smelled sweet and warm. He got the impression that she was much sweeter and warmer than she showed herself to be. He still couldn't figure her out. She was fun and bubbly, straightforward, and much more honest than most women he'd known—at least when it came to sex. He frowned. Now that he thought about it, she was happier to talk to about sex—to have sex—than she was to talk about feelings. That was the opposite of most women he'd known.

Did she really only see him that way? Was she only interested in sharing physical pleasure? He hoped not. The way she affected him might have come as a surprise, but he wanted to explore it. He'd meant what he'd told her last night. She'd pushed all thoughts of other women out of his head. As far as he was concerned, that was a big deal. He didn't intend to just let it go. She might think that he was only interested in spending a fun weekend with her, but he intended to win her over so that she, too, would be interested in more than that.

He wasn't going to question whether he'd be able to win her over. He didn't believe he was as egotistical as she liked to make out. He was simply realistic. He was a good guy, and he knew it. He could make her laugh; he was good company; he could make her moan. His interest stirred at the memory of how loudly she'd moaned last night.

She opened her eyes and looked up at him with a wry smile. Her fingers closed around him, and he closed his eyes.

"Good morning," she breathed.

He smiled back at her. "It is now."

She laughed. "Have you been waiting long?"

He raised an eyebrow.

"For me to wake up so that this guy," she stroked him as she said it, "can get to work?"

He smiled through pursed lips. "Is that all you think about? I was lying here thinking about you and me about spending more time together."

She chuckled. "Yeah, right. You say what you like, but this guy is giving away exactly what you were thinking we'd be doing in our time together."

He wanted to disagree, to tell her that he'd been thinking that sex was only a small part of it. But her warm hand wrapped around him was so persuasive—and it wasn't polite to disagree with a lady. Especially one who was rolling onto her back and edging her way underneath him.

He claimed her mouth in a kiss and slid his hand between her legs. Her hips moved in time with him as he stroked her. She was so responsive. She pumped her hand up and down the length of him. She knew how to work him. For a moment, he closed his eyes and relaxed into it. She could take him there in no time that way if she wanted to. If he let her. He didn't want to.

He nuzzled his face into her neck and pushed his fingers inside her. It worked. Both her arms came up around his back. He loved knowing that she was already wet for him. And, apparently, eager for more than his fingers. She was spreading her legs wide. Who was he to disagree?

He positioned himself above her and guided himself to her entrance. He wanted to thrust deep and hard, but having let her take control yesterday, he'd learned what she liked. She liked to go slow. He bit the inside of his cheek as he entered her slowly. It took every ounce of his willpower to go inch by inch, resisting the urge to drive his way home. He lifted his head and looked down into her eyes. Her cheeks and neck were flushed. Her fingers dug into his ass.

"Please?" she breathed.

No way could he resist that. He thrust his hips and was rewarded with a moan as they began to move together. She ran her nails over his shoulders, sending shivers racing down his spine. She was good—she knew what she was doing. He quickly chased that thought away. He didn't have room left for thoughts when she brought her legs up and wrapped them around his back, opening herself up for him to go deeper. Their bodies moved together frantically. The pressure was building at the base of his spine, ripples of pleasure radiated out from there with every thrust as she closed around him. He felt her start to tense and drove harder.

"Oh, oh, oh, God!"

Her orgasm took her, and she took him with her.

"Izzy!" He gasped as he let himself go in a whole-body orgasm that sent waves of pleasure crashing through him.

When they finally lay still, he cupped her cheek and looked deep into her eyes. Surely she must feel it, too?

"What are you doing to me?" he asked.

She chuckled. "I think it was you who did it to me, this time. But I'm not complaining."

He wanted to believe that there was something in her eyes, something that gave away the fact that yes, she felt it, too. But perhaps that was only wishful thinking. If she felt the same way he did, why would she avoid it?

She put a hand to his shoulder, and he rolled off her. Either she didn't feel it, or she was doing a good job of hiding it.

He couldn't resist closing his arms around her and pressing a kiss into her hair. He should be the one trying to move away afterward—trying to avoid any closeness—but she made him want to lie beside her just as much as he'd wanted to be inside her.

~ ~ ~

Izzy set her fork down and smiled. "You weren't kidding that you're a good cook, were you?"

He grinned at her. "I don't joke about important things. I wasn't kidding when I said I'll be happy to cook for you any time you like, either."

"Thank you." She knew what he was doing. He was taking every chance he got to let her know that he was serious. That he really was interested in the two of them starting to see each other. She let her gaze travel over him and tried to remember why she was so against the idea.

He smirked at her. "I appreciate the compliment, but I'm afraid I can't oblige just yet. You wore me out this morning, and we did just eat breakfast."

She laughed, realizing how brazen the look she'd given him must have appeared. "I'm sorry. I wasn't making suggestions. Just appreciating what I see."

He came to where she was still sitting at the island and put his hands on her hips. "So, you do understand that that look isn't always an invitation—or a *move* as you claim it is when I do it?"

She gave him a reluctant smile. "Okay, you win."

He shook his head. "I'm not trying to win points, Izzy. I'm hoping that I might break through and get you to understand where I'm coming from."

She held his gaze. She opened her mouth to shut him down, but then closed it again. What the hell was her problem here? Why did she keep doing that? She didn't even understand it herself. Okay, so he was a big macho guy, and she wasn't into guys like that. But was he? Really? Would he be standing in his kitchen after having made her breakfast if he were?

He looked concerned now. "I'm sorry. You want me to let it go?"

She searched his face. He would let it go if she told him to. He wasn't the kind of domineering prick that she'd judged him to be. He would let it go, and she knew that she'd regret it if he did.

She reached her hands up to cup his face and pulled him down to kiss her. He turned her insides to mush with his kisses. Why the hell wouldn't she just relax and enjoy it—enjoy him?

He looked puzzled when he lifted his head. "Are you resorting to kissing me to shut me up now?"

She laughed. "No! Though I can understand why you'd think that. I'm sorry, okay? I don't want you to let it go. I would like …" Was she really going to say it? Yes, she was. "I'd like to see what we might have going on between us."

His eyes twinkled when he smiled.

"I wish I could tell you why I'm so … so, whatever I've been toward you. I've told you before you're not my type, but that doesn't mean I don't find you attractive. It doesn't mean I don't like you or anything about you. I just … I'm just wary of big, macho, gorgeous men. I feel as though I'm just a game, and I don't want to be played."

"But I would never—"

She held her hand up to stop him. "I know you wouldn't. I prejudged you right from the get-go to be one of those guys. I accept that I was wrong … and I apologize."

He smiled and closed his arms around her. She rested her cheek against his chest and was surprised to hear his heart beating rapidly. "There's nothing to apologize for. I'm happy that you have revised your opinion of me." He looked down at her. "Now, do you want to get to know who I really am?"

She nodded. She already had a fair idea, and the Diego she was getting to know was a great guy.

Diego looked around the store. He was loving this. They'd come into town to walk around and browse the stores. He'd suggested that they should swim in the pool when they went home, but Izzy had refused since she hadn't brought a swimsuit.

He got the impression that he'd be able to persuade her to swim naked with him after dark, but for the afternoon, she needed a suit. And so, here he was, sitting outside the changing room while she tried some on.

He'd heard friends talk about the nightmare of shopping with their wives, about the tedium of sitting waiting while they tried on clothes. He hadn't experienced it before, though. When Zack's mother had still been in the picture, they hadn't had money or time to spare to go clothes shopping like this. And he'd never wanted to do it with anyone else.

The sales assistant smiled at him as he came back with another suit in a bigger size for Izzy.

"How are you doing in there?" Diego called.

"I'm fine. I think this one will do."

"May I see?"

She didn't answer.

He chuckled and exchanged a smile with the sales guy. "Is that a no?"

He heard her mutter something, and then the dressing room door opened. He sucked in a sharp breath. She looked amazing. The suit was a deep blue with white piping. It was gathered around the waist and tied between her breasts. He couldn't wait to untie that bow.

He heard her laugh. "I was going to ask what you think, but your face says it all."

"I—"

She laughed again. "Talk to me, not to them!"

He dragged his eyes away from her breasts and gave her a guilty smile. "You look amazing."

"Thank you." Her smile was different. Softer somehow. He felt like he was finally getting somewhere. He got to his feet and went to her. Putting his hands on her shoulders, he dropped a kiss on her lips. He couldn't help it.

She looked surprised but pleased.

The sales assistant smiled at them, and Izzy looked embarrassed. Diego didn't feel embarrassed. He didn't care who saw him kiss her.

"Well." She was flustered, and that surprised him. "I'd better get dressed, and we can get going."

She disappeared back into the changing room.

The sales assistant was still hovering, and Diego started to wonder if he should care about perhaps making the guy uncomfortable with his public display of affection. He gave him a rueful smile.

"Sorry about that."

The guy smiled back at him. "Don't be. It's nice to see older folks still in love. Believe me, I'm not going to judge anyone for kissing in public. I know too well how it feels to be on the receiving end of that kind of criticism."

Diego raised an eyebrow. He thought he understood, but he didn't want to assume.

The guy smiled and nodded. "My husband and I."

"I'm sorry." Diego shook his head sadly. "People can be assholes."

The guy smiled. "They can, but all we can do is try to focus on the ones who aren't."

Izzy came out and gave them a curious look. "Are we good to go?"

Diego nodded. He wanted to say something more to the guy, but he didn't know what.

The guy smiled back. "You two enjoy the rest of your day."

"Thanks," said Izzy. "You, too."

Diego did the only thing he could think of to show his appreciation. He held his hand out to shake and leaned in for a hug. "Thanks for all your help."

The guy hugged him back with a laugh. "My pleasure."

As they left the store, Izzy looked at Diego. He knew she was wondering what that had been about.

"What?" he raised an eyebrow.

"I guess I misjudged you again."

"I thought as much. You had me down as not just a macho guy with a big ego, but a homophobic, macho guy with a big ego?"

She nodded. "Sorry."

"You know that I'm hoping we're going to spend more time together, that we'll get to know each other better. If you do get to know me, you'll realize that I love diversity that allows diversity. The only people I have trouble tolerating are those who push for hate and intolerance. I try to understand others' ways of going about life. It can actually be a beautiful thing because it opens one up to more understanding and also knowledge about the world."

To his surprise, she reached up and planted a peck on his lips. "When you talk like that, you make me want to get to know you much better."

They walked hand in hand back to the car. Diego couldn't help smiling to himself. He was enjoying this. Izzy was good company. She was sharp and funny. He had brought dates to town in the past, but it'd felt as though he was doing it for them—to entertain them. He didn't feel that way with Izzy. They were just having fun, enjoying each other's company.

He squeezed her hand and smiled down at her. "Do you like it here?"

"You mean Laguna Beach?"

"Yes."

"I do. I hadn't been here for years, but it's a fun little town."

"Good. How would you feel about spending our weekends this way?"

Her smile disappeared. Damn. It seemed that perhaps he wasn't making as much progress as he'd thought. "You don't want to?"

She shook her head rapidly. "No. That's not what I meant. I told you, yes, I would like us to keep seeing each other. But you're not even going to be here most weekends, are you? You didn't buy a house in Summer Lake to let it sit idle while you hang out here with me. You need to be up there with your family."

"But I won't be there every weekend."

"Then, yes, I'd love to come and visit you on the weekends that you're here."

He had to wonder if she was being deliberately obtuse or whether he hadn't made himself clear enough yet. He frowned. "And what about the other weekends?"

"If you're questioning whether I'd still see other people on those weekends—"

He held his hand up to stop her. He knew her well enough to understand that she didn't want him—or anyone else—to dictate how or with whom she spent her time. "I wasn't questioning that. I was asking if you don't want to spend the other weekends with me, too."

"Oh." She looked so shocked that he had to drop a kiss on her lips. "Why are you so defensive, Miss Isobel?"

She shrugged.

"Is it me?"

"No. It's not. You've done nothing to make me doubt you." She gave him a rueful smile. "And so much to reassure me and get me to trust you. I'm sorry. I don't know why I'm so defensive."

He wasn't sure if he should risk it, but he had to know. "Are you reacting to your past? To your ex-husband?"

She shook her head rapidly. "No. It's not that. Tim's a nice guy. A good guy."

Diego nodded. He'd wondered if the ex was perhaps a big, macho guy who had mistreated her and left her determined not to go down the same road again.

"Someone else, then?"

She held his gaze for a moment and then looked away when they reached the car. "Kind of, but not in the way you think."

He unlocked the car and raised an eyebrow. He was giving her the choice. She could elaborate, or she could get in.

She opened the door. "If we're going to start seeing each other, then it'll all come out over time, won't it?"

He came around and got into the driver's seat. "I'll be patient. I can wait for you to tell me about your past." He leaned over and planted a kiss on her lips. "But I can't wait to explain what I was really asking. I want to know if you want to spend the other weekends with me, too." He waggled his eyebrows at her, hoping to see her smile again. "Why you think I would worry about you seeing other men is beyond me. No one could compete. You've found the best; the rest would only be pale imitations, now."

For a second, he thought she was about to tell him what an arrogant pig he was. Her eyes flashed, but then she burst out laughing. "I want to tell you that you're full of it. But you're not, are you? You're right. No one else could compete."

His heart felt as though it was buzzing in his chest. He grinned. "I'm glad we're finally on the same page. And just so you know, no one could compete with you either, Miss Isobel. You are the best ... for me."

He held her gaze, wondering if she'd have anything to say about that. She had no comebacks, though. She just looked deep into his eyes. What he saw in hers gave him hope.

# Chapter Eleven

Diego came and sat behind her on the sun lounger, and Izzy closed her eyes as he rubbed her shoulders. That felt so good. Everything felt so good. This whole weekend had been wonderful. He'd taken her out to dinner last night, and afterward, they'd gone dancing and then walked on the beach in the darkness.

When they'd come home, he'd made love to her again. A shiver ran down her back at the memory. He was amazing in bed. He slid his arms around her waist and pulled her back against his chest. "Are you all right?"

She nodded happily. "I'm wonderful."

"I agree." He nuzzled his lips into her neck. At first, she'd thought that was a calculated move—calculated because he knew the effect it would have on her. Now, she saw it differently. It wasn't Diego trying to turn her on because he wanted to sleep with her. It was Diego expressing affection because, as he'd told her, that was just who he was. She smiled. And having sex with her was only one of the many ways he liked to express his affection.

"What time do you need to be home?"

Her smile faded. He was right. She needed to think about it, but she didn't want to. She had to go home and get started on this new chapter of her life—the chapter where she didn't have an office to go to anymore, and she didn't have her best friend.

She looked up at him over her shoulder. She wouldn't have Diego once she got home either. She believed him when he said that he wanted to start seeing her, but she didn't know how often it would happen. He was thrilled at the prospect of being closer to his son—he might say he wanted her to go with him, but that was about family. She wasn't part of it. The only family she'd been part of was Audrey's.

He dropped a kiss on her nose. "You're not going to tell me? Am I supposed to guess?"

"Sorry." He'd asked what time she needed to be home. "It doesn't matter. Whatever's easy for you and Karl."

He held her tighter and rested his chin on her shoulder. "In that case, you can stay here. That would be easier for Karl; he won't have to fly. And it will be so much easier for me than having to say goodbye to you. I don't want to do that."

A warm feeling swept through her, and she turned to kiss his cheek. If she took him at his word, he might possibly be the sweetest man she'd ever known. All the things he said that she'd believed were lines were just him expressing his feelings—and being honest about them. "I'll be sad to say goodbye to you, too." She wanted him to know that.

"So, don't go."

She sighed. "I have to. I have work to do, and I'm sure you do as well."

He nibbled her neck, and his hand came up and closed around her breast. "Can I try to persuade you to stay?"

"No." She had to say no because she knew that he wouldn't have to try too hard.

He sighed, but his fingers slid inside her swimsuit to tease her nipple. "Okay, then. I'll take you home. But can I try to persuade you to come back next weekend?"

"Mmm."

He rolled her nipple between his finger and thumb. "Is that a yes?"

"Mmm."

"I need you to say yes, Miss Isobel."

She smiled. "Then you're going to have to make me." She'd screamed yes, very enthusiastically a few times this weekend. If he wanted another one, he knew how to get it.

~ ~ ~

Diego watched her gather her things. He didn't want her to go home, but he knew that she felt she had to. He was hoping that this might work the same way as the first night they'd met. He'd wanted more then, but he'd known he wouldn't get it by pushing for it. Instead, he'd left her wanting him. It'd taken a while, but she'd eventually admitted that she wanted more, too.

He had gotten her to agree—very loudly—that she wanted to spend next weekend with him. He wanted to take her to the lake. He had the impression that she wasn't too keen to go up there. But it didn't matter. What mattered was that they spent time together—not where.

She set her bag down next to the island and picked up her purse. "Ready when you are."

He didn't get the chance to reply before her phone rang. She frowned and took it out of her purse to check it.

"Hmm. I need to take this. I won't be long, but it's Audrey."

He nodded.

"Hey, girlfriend. How are you settling in? ... Yeah? ... That's great ... No ... No. I'm fine ... Nothing's wrong."

Diego wondered if she was avoiding telling her friend that she was here with him.

She smiled at him through pursed lips and shook her head. "If you must know, I'm at Diego's house. I've been here all weekend." She laughed and met his gaze. "Yes. I think it's awesome, too. He's really not the asshole I thought he was."

Diego laughed and held his hand out for the phone.

She arched an eyebrow at him and then handed it over.

"Hello, lovely Audrey."

"Hi, Diego! I'm so happy! I didn't know if you were making a big mistake going back to the restaurant like that on Friday afternoon."

He grinned at Izzy. "I knew it was not a mistake. I knew that Miss Isobel would not be able to resist me if she just gave me a chance." He let his eyes travel over. "She opened up to me."

Izzy rolled her eyes at that.

"And now we are ..."

Izzy snatched the phone back out of his hand. "His ego is as big as I thought it was, though. Perhaps bigger."

He couldn't resist, he closed his arms around her and pressed himself against her ass.

She laughed and added. "To be fair, though. I understand a bit better now why he's so full of himself."

He laughed with her and whispered next to her ear. "And you don't mind being full of me."

Her eyes widened, but she smiled and nodded happily before she spoke into the phone again. "Okay. I'll talk to you in the morning. I'm heading home now, anyway ... No ... No ... I'll talk to you tomorrow."

~ ~ ~

When they landed at the Santa Paula airport, Diego carried her bag through the airport building and out to her car for her. He kept his arm around her shoulders as they crossed the parking lot.

She took the bag from him and threw it onto the back seat, then looked up into his eyes and smiled. "Thank you."

He cupped his hands around the sides of her neck and looked down at her lips. She knew what was coming. She loved the way he kissed her. He trapped her body against the car and claimed her mouth. It was a gentler kiss than she'd grown used to from him. It left her clinging to him, wishing that this wasn't goodbye.

When he lifted his head, his eyes were full of tenderness. "I could come with you—cook dinner for you."

She chuckled. "I'd love that. But we both know you need to go home. You have to go to work tomorrow, and so do I."

He nodded sadly. "Okay. If you insist that I must go, then I must go. But you won't forget your promise?"

She'd promised him that she'd see him next weekend. "I won't forget, but I won't hold you to it if your plans change."

He frowned.

"Come on, Diego. I know you'll want to go to the lake. You need to see Zack, and I'm sure you'll need to do stuff with your new house and everything." She slid her arms around his waist, wanting him to understand that she wasn't giving him the brush off, just giving him an easy out if he figured out that he wanted one.

He held her to him and rested his chin on top of her head. "I want to see you. I'll come and get you just as soon as you say I can, okay?"

She nodded.

"Would you mind if we went to the lake?"

"I wouldn't, but I understand that going up there is about going to see your son. It's about family, and I don't want to encroach on that time. That's special."

He leaned back and looked down into her eyes. "It is. I won't deny that. And I love that you respect it."

There, she was relieved that he'd admitted it, even if it did leave her out in the cold. It was worth it. She might not be part of one, but she knew that family came first.

"I need you to understand that you're special, too, Miss Isobel." He searched her face.

She didn't know what to say to that. She wanted to make a joke, but the look in his eyes stopped her.

He tucked his fingers under her chin and planted a kiss on her lips. "You don't believe me yet, but you will. You are a very special lady."

She hugged him tighter and rested her cheek against his chest again. She wasn't so much avoiding his gaze as trying to avoid admitting just how special she thought he was, too.

He let go of her and stepped back. "I believe it's time to say goodbye."

She nodded. She didn't want to. She wished they could at least stand here a little longer. She already missed the way his arms felt around her.

He ducked his head and planted one last kiss on her lips.

"Goodbye, Izzy."

She nodded, hoping that this wasn't going to turn out to be a real goodbye.

He turned and started to walk away, then stopped and looked back. "May I call you to say goodnight?"

She smiled and nodded.

"I'll talk to you later, then."

When the plane touched down, Diego's phone buzzed with a message. He smiled when he saw a voicemail from Ted. He'd wondered how long that would take after Audrey spoke to Izzy.

He listened to it while Karl taxied back to the FBO building.

"Hey. It sounds as though going to Ventura with me on Friday afternoon worked out well for you. Audrey says that Izzy spent the whole weekend with you. Give me a call when you get a chance. I want to hear all about it."

He smiled. He'd talk to Ted later. For now, he tapped out a text to Izzy.

*Tell me I don't have to wait until next weekend?*

He watched the screen for a few moments, willing her to answer. Hoping that she might be eager to see him again sooner than that.

She didn't reply.

He put his phone away when Karl came out of the cockpit and let down the steps.

"Do you have anything on the schedule this week?" Diego asked.

"No. It's looking quiet … unless you have anything coming up?"

"I might. I'll give you a call in the morning."

Karl smiled. "Okay. Would I be crazy to think that we might be heading back to Ventura?"

Diego laughed. "Only as crazy as I am to hope so."

"I don't think you're crazy. I think Izzy's awesome."

"She is."

"I liked her from that first weekend we brought her back here." He frowned. "Mind if I ask you what happened? That was a long while ago now."

Diego shrugged. "She was worth waiting for."

"Is this serious then?"

"It's starting to look that way."

"Wow. I thought you and Ted were confirmed bachelors, and now, here you both are meeting women and moving to Summer Lake."

Diego looked at him. Was that what he was doing? Was he going down the same road that Ted had taken with Audrey? He smiled at the realization that he'd like to. But then he had to wonder if that was something Izzy would even consider.

All he could do was hope so.

# Chapter Twelve

Izzy poured herself a drink and took it outside to sit by the pool. Well! She'd sure enjoyed her weekend. She smiled as she thought about Diego. In some ways, he was exactly what she'd believed him to be. He was big and sexy as sin. He was a charmer, no two ways about it. She chuckled, and he was a sex hound, too! She really needed to come up with a different word for it. He might not be chasing everything in a skirt, but there was no denying that he was a man who liked sex. Especially, it seemed sex with her.

Not that she was complaining. She was a woman who liked sex. Especially sex with him. He was amazing. He knew what he was doing, but more than that, he seemed to understand what she wanted, too.

She jumped when her phone beeped with a text. When she checked it, she had a couple of them, and a voicemail, too.

The first text was from Rafa.

*I stopped by to see you, but you weren't home.*

*Do you want to get together this week?*

She made a face. No, she didn't. At least, not with him. She had the feeling that she'd spend every evening—and night—wishing that she could get together with Diego, but her days—and nights—with Rafa were behind her.

*I don't. Thanks, Rafa, but it's time we let it go.*

She thought they had let it go. She'd seen him a couple of times in the last few months, but they hadn't slept together. They'd gone for a drink, but that was all.

*Can I come over? Can we talk about it?*

She made a face. It wasn't as though there was anything that needed to be said. They used to sleep together—now, they didn't anymore.

*No. I've had a long weekend. I'm tired.*

*We're good, right? Still friends?*

He was a sweet guy, but he wasn't for her. She'd been upfront with him from the beginning. It surprised her that she needed to be. It seemed that guys these days were a lot more clingy and needy than she'd expect them to be. A few of the younger guys she'd dated had acted as though they wanted to get into something with her—some kind of relationship. All she wanted was a few laughs and a good time in bed.

*Still friends. Still hoping for more.*

She blew out a sigh.

*Not going to happen, sweetie. Goodnight.*

She checked her other messages. There was a voicemail from Audrey, who, no doubt, wanted to hear all about her and Diego. And there was a text from him, too! She smiled as she clicked on it.

*Tell me I don't have to wait until next weekend?*

She pressed her lips together. She'd rather he didn't. She'd felt as though she had to come home just to get her balance back. She'd gotten all swept up in him—in them—over the course of the weekend. She needed to step back and get right with herself before this went any further. But he'd only left her a couple of hours ago, and she was already wishing that she'd brought him home with her. Not just in the traditional sense of bringing a guy home—though she wouldn't deny that she'd love some more of him. But she wished he was still with her. He was such good company. He was fun, yes, but more than that, he was intelligent and attentive. She blew out a sigh and looked at the text again. She wanted to tell him that no, they didn't have to wait. But she'd come home to try to clear her head and see how she felt when she wasn't totally intoxicated by the man.

She'd answer him in a little while. First, she wanted to call Audrey.

She dialed her number and waited.

"Hello, you! Are you home?"

"I am."

"Oh."

"Oh, what?"

"I just had this feeling that you might not go home, that you might stay with Diego."

Izzy laughed. "He asked me to. I wanted to."

"So, why didn't you?"

"I don't know, Audrey. I feel as though I'm drowning in a sea of Diego. I need a little time to get my head above water and figure out what's going on."

"I think I can tell you what's going on."

"I think I know what you're going to say."

"And you don't want to hear it?"

"Not yet. I think you might be right, but I don't want to hear it yet, okay?"

"Okay. So, what happens next?"

"I don't know."

"The two of you didn't make any more plans?"

"Not exactly."

"Oh." Audrey sounded disappointed.

"Don't worry. We've said we're going to see each other next weekend."

"Great, then that's what happens next, isn't it?"

Izzy chuckled. "Maybe, depending on how I answer the text he just sent."

"Saying what?"

"Asking if he has to wait until next weekend."

Audrey laughed. "Well, we both know the answer to that."

"I guess we do. But anyway, tell me about you? How was your weekend? How are the kids settling in? I'll bet they're glad that you're finally up there with them now, aren't they?"

"They are. They're doing great. Ally has a whole bunch of weddings lined up now, and Brayden's loving his new job. They both came over for lunch today, and Ted's son Eddie and his fiancée April came, too. It was wonderful. They both said they missed you, though."

"Tell them I miss them, too. But this is how it goes, Audrey. You guys are patching together your new family. You don't need me in the way for that."

"You're not in the way, Iz. You're part of the family. I wish you'd get that through your head once and for all."

Izzy shrugged.

"I'm going to say something, and you might think I'm crazy."

"That'll make a nice change from you thinking I am."

"True. But listen, Iz. I have a feeling that you and Diego are going to get serious soon."

Izzy wanted to laugh, but she didn't. It did sound crazy, but for some ridiculous reason, it didn't feel crazy—it didn't feel crazy at all.

"And if you do, you're going to need to get used to the idea of being part of a family."

She pressed her lips together. "Diego and Zack have each other. They missed out on a lot of years by the sounds of it. Now, they want to make up for lost time. It's different when there's just two guys. They just need their time together, and that's it. No big deal about family or being part of it."

"I think you're wrong about that. I think family is very important to Diego. He just hasn't been able to have one. Now he has Zack back, and Zack has Maria. And I think he'll want his own lady to be a central part of his family."

Izzy didn't say anything. She knew Audrey was right. That was why she'd skirted around the idea of going to Summer

Lake with him. She didn't want to encroach on his family time. And … and she didn't dare believe that he might want her to be part of it. That was the truth.

"Are you okay?" asked Audrey.

"Yeah. You know how screwed up I am over the whole family thing."

"I do. That's why I'm mentioning it now."

"Thanks, Audrey. It might not even be an issue, though."

"Maybe not. But we both believe that it will, don't we?"

Izzy sighed. "Yep. I have to tell you. He is freaking amazing. I thought he was so full of it. I thought he was spouting crap just to get me into bed."

Audrey laughed. "And now you can see that he's just a romantic, saying beautiful things and sweeping you off your feet?"

"Yeah. I suppose that's it."

"Well, now you can see it, I hope you can relax and enjoy it? I think most women would give their right arm to be in the position you find yourself in with him."

"I won't make you blush and talk about positions but err … yeah!"

Audrey laughed. "Hey. I know you thought I lived a sheltered life when I was married, and after the divorce, but I can tell you I've learned a thing or two in the last few months myself."

"I'm happy to hear it—but I don't need to hear all about it, thank you. Anyway, had I better let you get back to Ted?"

"That's okay. He's on the phone, too. I think Diego called him."

Izzy had to laugh. "This should feel weird. That I'm talking to you and he's talking to Ted, but it doesn't. In fact, I kind of like it."

"I do, too. Oh, actually, I have another call coming in, it's Ally. I'd better take it."

"Of course. Tell her I said hi. I'll talk to you in the morning."

As she set her phone down, she wondered what Diego was saying to Ted. She could see that their friendship was similar to the one she and Audrey shared, and she liked that about him. In her experience, men didn't usually have such close friends.

She picked up her phone again and looked at his text.

*Tell me I don't have to wait until next weekend?*

She didn't want him to wait. If she was honest, she was wishing that she hadn't even come home. But that was crazy thinking. They'd had a wonderful weekend, but that didn't mean it wouldn't wear thin if she stayed for longer. She knew that for her, and she'd guess that for him, too, the last couple of days were the longest time she'd spent with someone on a date. He probably took his other women out for dinner before he took them to bed—he was a gentleman, she had to give him that. She frowned at the thought of him with other women. She didn't like that. It shouldn't bother her, but it did.

Wasn't that something? She wasn't into exclusivity herself. She didn't want someone restricting her that way. She pursed her lips. At least, she hadn't wanted it. Now, it seemed that she did. She loved the idea of Diego wanting her all for himself. And she wanted him all for herself. How about that?

She tapped out a reply.

*We don't have to wait till next weekend.*

She hit send and waited. He might not see it for a while. He might be on the phone with Ted still. Apparently, he wasn't.

*Thank you. What time are you going to bed?*

She smiled. He really was sweet.

*Probably around eleven.*

His reply came almost immediately.

*Ok. Can I talk to you at 10:30?*

She wouldn't be surprised if they ended up having phone sex before she went to sleep.

*I'll look forward to it.*

His reply came in the form of a big red heart followed by:

*Not as much as I am.*

~ ~ ~

Diego pulled the rental car over to the side of the road a few houses down from Izzy's. He couldn't help smiling to himself as he took out his phone. It was 10:25 p.m. He'd wait and call her at 10:30 p.m. on the dot.

There was, of course, the chance that she wouldn't be pleased to see him. But he didn't believe it was much of a chance. She'd felt the same way he had when he'd left her at the airport earlier. He knew it.

He'd thought that maybe he would show up here tomorrow night—that he could bring groceries and make her dinner. But he hadn't been able to wait. When he'd gotten home, he'd talked to Ted and to Zack; they were both enthusiastic about him having spent the weekend with her.

When she'd finally texted him back that he didn't have to wait until the weekend to see her again, he'd called Karl to see if he'd be able to fly again tonight or tomorrow.

Then when he'd hung up, he'd received a message from Austin, the realtor in Summer Lake telling him that he should be able to close on the house on Friday. That had sealed it for him.

He wanted to close as soon as possible, but he also wanted to spend the weekend with Izzy. He was going to need some time to convince her that she should go up there with him—and there was no time like the present to get started.

He smiled as he looked at the contacts in his phone. Zack had been number one on his speed dial ever since he'd had a phone. Ted was number two. He pursed his lips as he thought about it, then nodded to himself. He added Izzy's number at number one, and the others each moved down a place. It felt right.

He dialed and then waited.

She answered on the second ring.

"Hello!"

Just the sound of her voice made him smile. "*Hola, mi amor.*"

"Ooh! I like the sound of that!"

He laughed.

"Why didn't I think of this before? I can get you to talk dirty to me in Spanish."

"Will you understand what I'm saying?" He had to wonder if she knew what he'd just said, or if she was choosing not to question it.

"I won't have a freaking clue, but it won't matter. It sounds so sexy."

"Good to know. I'll remember that and use it when I can."

"You can use it right now if you like. I'm in bed already."

He smiled to himself. Did she think that was all this phone call was about? She kept calling him a sex hound, but she was the one who made everything about sex. "And what are you expecting from me?"

She laughed. "You know damned well what I'm expecting. You asked if we could talk before bedtime."

"I did."

"Are you going to tell me that you don't want to talk about the kind of things that we've been doing at bedtime for the last couple of nights?"

"I am." He started the car and drove the last short distance to her house.

"Oh." She sounded confused.

"Aren't you going to ask me why I don't want to talk about it?" He pulled into the driveway and flashed the headlights.

"I am, but hang on a minute."

He smirked to himself, imagining her getting out of bed to see what was going on. He cut the engine, and when he saw the curtains move, he got out of the car and smiled up at her.

"What the …? What are you doing here?"

He laughed. "I couldn't stay away. I had to see you again. But I'll leave if you want me to."

The curtain closed, and he heard her laugh. "Don't you dare go anywhere! I'll be right down."

The front door flew open, and she stood there smiling at him. She looked more beautiful than ever in a pair of shorts and a tank top. He was thrilled when she ran out into the driveway and threw her arms around his neck. He held her close to his chest and looked down into her eyes.

If he'd had any doubts about whether she might feel the same way he did, he found his answer in the way she smiled up at him.

He cupped her cheek in his hand and claimed her mouth in a kiss that let her know just how happy he was to see her again.

When they came up for air, she took his hand and led him inside. "I can't believe you're here." She looked up at him. "Did you go home and come back again?"

He nodded happily.

"I'll bet Karl hates me?"

He had to laugh at that. "If you did, you'd lose. Karl thinks you're wonderful. He told me so, and he also asked me why it's taken me so long to win you over."

She raised an eyebrow at him.

"I couldn't tell him why." He held her gaze for a moment. "I'm hoping that you'll tell me why. I'm happy that I'm finally making progress at winning your heart, but I want to know what's held you back ... what holds you back."

She didn't look thrilled at the question, and he knew better than to push it. Instead, he closed his arms around her and kissed her again. He could take his time, but he knew that before he could ask her to move forward with him, he'd have to understand her better.

She reached up and sank her fingers in his hair. "There's nothing holding me back right now. I have a warm bed and a gorgeous man." She looked into his eyes. "You're not going to hold back on me, are you?"

He wasn't. He slid his hands inside her shorts, and the feel of her bare ass had him pressing himself against her as she kissed him. They needed to talk, but talking could wait. As she took his hand and led him upstairs, he knew that this couldn't wait.

# Chapter Thirteen

Izzy sniffed the air and smiled. Damn, the man hadn't been joking when he'd told her he was a good cook. He'd arrived back at her place a while ago loaded down with grocery bags.

She'd been concerned because she wasn't done with work yet. She smiled as she remembered the way he'd kissed her and then patted her ass and told her to get back to it while he made them dinner.

It was hard to concentrate on work, knowing that he was in her kitchen. But she was almost done now. Her phone rang, and she frowned at it. She didn't want to answer. She wanted the workday to be over and for her evening with Diego to begin.

She smiled when she saw that it was Audrey.

"Hey," she answered.

"Hi. How's it going?"

"Great. I'm almost done for the day."

Audrey laughed. "I should think so."

"Why's that?"

"Because I know he's there with you."

Izzy hadn't mentioned that Diego was here. She and Audrey had spoken several times throughout the day, but it was about work. And she didn't want Audrey to think that she was slacking in her first week working from home. "He hasn't been here all day. He went to work for a few hours, and then he went to the grocery store … and now he's making us dinner!"

"I know. He talked to Ted. I heard all about it. What I want to know is how you're feeling?"

Izzy pursed her lips.

"Uh-oh. Is it too much for you?"

"No! I'm not staying quiet because I'm uncomfortable with it. I think I'm just shocked at myself at how much I'm loving it."

"Oh, Iz. That's wonderful. And you know, if you want to take some time off, you go ahead. We're not exactly busy at the moment."

"No! No way. I mean, thanks for the offer, but if he's going to be a part of my life, then he's going to have to fit into my life, isn't he?"

"Oh, my goodness! I was hoping things might be headed in that direction, but I didn't expect to hear you admit it just yet."

"Admit what?"

"That he's going to be part of your life."

Izzy looked over her shoulder. She was upstairs in the spare room that she'd converted into an office. Diego was downstairs in the kitchen. He was hardly likely to overhear, but she still felt self-conscious admitting it.

"Are you going to clam up on me now?" asked Audrey.

She chuckled. "No. I'm not. I'm just making sure that he's not around to hear me when I tell you that it feels like he already is part of my life—and I like it!"

"Wow, Izzy! That's wonderful! Oh, I'm so happy for you."

"Don't get carried away. It might all wear off as fast as it happened."

"Do you really think so?"

"No. I don't. But I'm not sure I can trust just yet that this is as real—as special—as it feels."

"Aww, Izzy. Please try? He's a wonderful guy. Of course, there are no guarantees, but ... well, maybe there are? You can guarantee that it won't work out if you don't give it the chance to."

Izzy sighed. "Aren't you the wise one?"

"Just hopeful. Hopeful that you and Diego might find the same kind of thing Ted and I have."

Izzy frowned. Audrey and Ted were in love—they were going to get married. She'd sworn off that four-letter word years ago.

"Are you still there?"

"Yep."

"Have I spooked you?"

She thought about it for a long moment. "Not spooked me, no. But you've given me food for thought."

"Is that good or bad?"

She smiled. "Good. I've been a confirmed cynic for far too long. But you know what? Thinking that I might have the chance to be as happy as you are ...? That Diego and I could possibly ..." She didn't even dare say it out loud. "Well, it feels ... good."

"Then get off the phone. Shut down for the day, and go enjoy your evening with him. And if you want to take the week off, then do it. Okay? We're hardly busy, are we?"

"I'm not going to take the week, but ..."

Audrey laughed. "You do whatever feels right, just know that whatever you choose is great with me."

"Thanks, Audrey."

"You are more than welcome."

After she hung up, Izzy stared out the window. It felt as though all her resistance to Diego and to being with him was melting away. She hugged her arms around her chest and smiled. Ever since she and Tim had divorced, she'd been wary of men—at least of getting into relationships. She didn't usually let herself dwell on the end of her marriage. Audrey used to tell her that she perhaps needed to work her way through her feelings, but eight years had gone by now. That was the past. It was sad, but she'd dealt with much worse than that.

She heard Diego's footsteps on the stairs and smiled when he popped his head around the door.

"Sorry. I don't mean to disturb you ..."

She held her arms out to him, and he came in with a smile.

"But I'll be happy to ... if you're finished?"

She nodded happily. "I just talked to Audrey. I'm done for the day." She got to her feet and felt a wave of warmth and happiness rush through her when he closed his arms around her.

"Excellent. Then do you want to come and keep me company while I finish dinner?"

"I do. But tell me what I can do to help? I don't need to sit on my ass the whole time while you wait on me."

He chuckled. "You don't need to do a thing. It's almost ready." His smile faded, and he looked thoughtful. It seemed that he really did understand her when he added. "But I'll take a drink if you're offering. And I don't know where you want to eat? You could set the table if you want to … inside or out?"

She smiled. She wasn't one to sit around while someone else did for her. She hated when a man expected her to take care of him, and she didn't need one to take care of her either.

Once she had the table set out on the deck by the pool, she went back inside to join him in the kitchen. He handed her a glass of wine, and she took it with a smile. "Thank you."

"Thank you for letting me stick around, for letting me make dinner for you."

She went to him and closed her arms around his waist. "I love that you want to make dinner. I love that you want to stick around."

He cupped his hands around the sides of her neck and looked down at her lips. Her tummy flipped over, knowing what was coming. She couldn't get enough of the way he kissed her.

He looked up into her eyes again, and his words stole her breath away. "I love you, Miss Isobel."

Her heart started to pound, and her stomach felt like it was doing backflips. She opened her mouth to speak, but his lips came down on hers, and the way he kissed her left no room for doubt that what he'd said wasn't just words.

When he finally lifted his head, he raised an eyebrow at her. He wasn't asking her to say it back, at least. He was asking if it was okay that he'd said it. Her heart still felt as though it might beat its way out of her chest, but she was sagging against him, letting him hold her up, loving the way his arms felt around her. She nodded slowly. It *was* okay that he'd said it. It was okay—much more than just okay that he felt that way—it was amazing. But it had been such a long time since she'd even contemplated the possibility that she might ever feel that way again. She pressed her lips together.

He planted a peck on the tip of her nose and turned away to stir one of the pans. "Don't look so worried. I don't need to hear you say it. Not yet, anyway. I simply need you to know how I feel. So that you can think about it." He turned back around and smiled at her. "So, that you can get used to the idea."

She had to smile back at him. His confidence was irresistible, and she had to admit that it was a big part of his charm.

He came back to stand before her and put his hands on her shoulders. "Do you think you might be able to get used to the idea?"

She nodded slowly, and a smile spread across her face. He might have taken her by surprise; it might feel like it had come out of nowhere, but if she was honest, she was already getting used to the idea that he could fall for her—that she could fall for him.

~ ~ ~

Diego checked the clock on the dashboard when he pulled into the parking lot at the airport. He was early. Karl was taking him back to Laguna Beach at six-thirty. He had to spend a couple of hours in the office this morning, and he needed to stop at the house to pick up more clothes to take to the lake.

The week had flown by—he'd spent most of it at Izzy's place. He'd slept there every night with her. He'd come back into the office every day except Wednesday. And now that the weekend was here, she'd agreed to come up to the lake with him. Austin had everything set to close on the house this afternoon.

He pulled out his phone. It was early, but he knew that Austin was an early riser. Still, he sent a text rather than calling.

*Are the sellers happy with the separate bill of sale on the furniture?*

*And am I coming to your office at three?*

The reply came back almost immediately.

*Yes, on the furniture and the time. No on the location. The closing is at the title office. Do you want me to pick you up?*

Diego frowned.

*Do I have the address?*

It made him smile that each reply came back almost instantaneously.

*It's at 48, Main St. 100 yards past the bakery if you're heading out of the resort.*

He thought about it for a moment.

*I'll see you there just before three.*

Austin came back one last time.

*I'll be there at 2:45. Call me if you have any questions beforehand.*

Diego put his phone away with a smile. He liked Austin. He was one of Zack's friends. It seemed that all his friends up at the lake were good kids. He pursed his lips at that. They weren't kids. They were all in their thirties, getting married, and starting families of their own. He hoped that Zack and Maria would hurry up and start their family soon. He couldn't wait to be a grandpa.

His smile faded as a thought hit him. He had to wonder if that wasn't part of Izzy's hesitation over being part of a family.

She didn't have any. She didn't have children, and therefore, would never have grandchildren. His smile was back at the thought that if things went the way he hoped they would between the two of them, then she'd be a grandma to Zack's kids, too.

He looked around the parking lot, feeling a little self-conscious about getting so carried away. He knew he probably shouldn't be thinking this way about a woman who hadn't even told him she loved him—yet. She'd probably say it was just his big ego, but he knew in his heart that if she didn't feel that way about him yet, it was only a matter of time until she did.

He hit the speed dial on his phone. He knew that Zack would be up.

"*Hola, Papá. Qué pasa?*"

"*Hola, mi hijo.* I wanted to check in with you. What are your plans this weekend?"

"Not much. We want to go to the Boathouse tomorrow night because everyone's out. Of course, we're hoping that includes you. Other than that, I'm waiting to hear what your plans are."

"I just talked with Austin. The closing is at three this afternoon."

"That's awesome, Papá. I can't believe that after all these years we're finally going to be living just down the road from each other. Well, I know you won't exactly be living there—"

"What would you think if I did?"

"Did what? Actually lived here? I'd love it! You know that. Is that what you're thinking?"

"I'm starting to."

"Tell me to butt out if you like, but what about Izzy? I was thinking that she might be a reason for you to keep spending more time at the beach."

Diego smiled to himself. "I want to ask her to come with me."

Zack was quiet for a few moments. It was long enough to make Diego's smile fade.

"You don't like the idea?"

"I do. It's just …"

"What? You think it's too soon?"

"No. Not really. Not if it's what you want."

"It is."

"And is it what she wants?"

"I hope so."

"I hope so, too. Sorry. I should have sounded more enthusiastic. I guess I'm just feeling a little protective."

Diego had to laugh at that. "Of me—or of her?"

Zack didn't laugh with him. "Of you, of course. I mean, from what I saw of her, she seemed nice enough. But at the same time … don't take this the wrong way, she didn't seem like the type who was looking to settle down. She's not like Audrey, is she?"

Diego mulled that over before he spoke again. Zack had a point. But his smile was back when it hit him. "No, she's not like Audrey. But then I'm not like Ted, either. And until I met Izzy, you would hardly have described me as the type who was looking to settle down."

Zack laughed. "You're right about that. It's the last thing I expected of you. But if that's what you want—and what she wants, then I'm behind you all the way."

"Thanks, mi hijo."

"There's nothing to thank me for. I love you. I want to see you happy. Whatever—whoever—makes you happy is good by me. So, do we get to spend some time with her this weekend? You know Maria's going to want to get to know her ... she's probably as protective of you as I am."

Diego chuckled at that. "She is. And I love her for it. I'll tell you what, do you guys want to come over to the house tomorrow afternoon?"

"Sure. That'll be great."

"Okay. We'll see you then."

"Can I ask you something before you go?"

"Anything."

"Are you in love with her?"

Diego grinned. "I am."

"And is she in love with you?"

"I believe she is. She just doesn't know it yet."

Zack didn't laugh at that like he'd hoped he would. "Okay. Will you guys be out tonight?"

"I don't know yet. I'll give you a call."

"Okay. Love you, Papá."

"Love you."

Diego hung up with a wry smile. He'd hoped Zack might be a little more enthusiastic about his confession that he'd fallen in love with Izzy, but he could understand his caution. He'd feel the same way if the roles were reversed. Still, it'd be different once he got to know her. He'd understand then.

# Chapter Fourteen

"So, tell me all about it?" Audrey asked with a smile.

Izzy smiled back at her. "I don't know where to start."

"Anywhere you like. You know, you haven't even told me what actually happened when he came back for you after we left Ventura. You've only given me snippets since then."

Izzy blew out a sigh but couldn't help grinning as she remembered how shocked she'd been when she saw Diego walking back out onto the terrace at the restaurant after he'd left with Audrey and Ted.

Audrey laughed. "That smile tells me it's quite a story."

Izzy looked up when the server came out with their drinks. Audrey had come over to meet her at the lodge at Four Mile Creek. Diego had asked if she wanted to go into town with him, but he was going to the title office to close on his house, and she hadn't wanted to be in the way.

When the server had gone, she picked up her drink. "I couldn't believe that he'd come back. Honestly, I was sitting there feeling a little bit sorry for myself, you know. You'd just gone off to start your new life here with Ted. And ..." She stopped when she saw Audrey's face. "Don't look like that ... I'm thrilled for you ... you know I am. But I miss you."

"Well, if this goes the way it's starting to look like it will, you won't have to miss me for long."

Izzy's heart rate picked up. She kept wondering how all this was going to work out. She knew what Diego wanted. She'd be lying if she said she didn't like the idea, but …

Audrey raised an eyebrow at her. "What's wrong?"

"Nothing. What could be wrong? He's wonderful, and he cares about me." She met her friend's gaze and decided to tell her. The two of them told each other everything. "He says he loves me, Audrey."

Audrey clapped her hands together. "Oh, Iz! That's wonderful! … Isn't it?"

She nodded slowly. "It is."

"But?"

"But nothing. I mean, come on. He's a great guy. He's gorgeous." She waggled her eyebrows. "He's amazing in bed."

"But? It still feels like there's a but. What are you not saying?"

She shrugged. "I don't know. Well, I do know. What I'm not saying, at least, not to him, is that I love him, too."

"But you do?"

She nodded again.

"So, why haven't you told him?"

"Because I promised myself that I wouldn't ever go there again."

"I know, but that was a long time ago. Things are different now." Audrey touched her arm. "It's not as though he's looking to have kids, is it?"

She blew out a sigh. "No. It isn't. We're too old for that even if we wanted to."

"So, don't you think it's time to let it go?"

"Yeah. I know it is. I just need to get used to it. I need a bit of time. And come on, even you can admit that this is all happening too fast."

"Do you think so? You've known him for months. You've known him for as long as I've known Ted."

"I met him months ago, but it's not as though we've spent much time together. I hardly saw him for a couple of months there."

"True, but you can't deny that you thought about him a lot in that time. Ted brought it up the other day, and he's right. From the day Diego met you, he didn't even date anyone else—and you didn't either."

"I went out with Rafa a couple of times."

Audrey made a face. "You went out with him, but you didn't sleep with him."

"I know. Isn't that weird? If you'd told me at the time that it was because of Diego, I would have laughed at you."

"And now?"

"Now, it doesn't seem so funny."

"Why?"

She had to smile. "It's not funny because it makes me have to admit that this is serious."

Audrey grinned. "Oh, I hope it is. I really do. The two of you are perfect together. I can see you moving up here and we can work together again and—"

Izzy held her hand up. "I can see it, too, but don't you think it's too fast?"

"No. I really don't. And you surprise me that you keep going back to that. You were all about me getting together with Ted, and that happened a lot faster than this. What's the real problem?"

"I don't know."

"You don't know, or you don't want to say?"

"I … I don't know, Audrey." She blew out a sigh. "Okay, I do know. But I feel stupid."

"Well, you're not stupid. So, why don't you just tell me, and I'll help you work your way past it?"

"Thanks."

Audrey waited with her eyebrows raised.

"Things just don't work out this well for me. They really don't. I don't want to let myself believe it because I'll only end up hurt and disappointed."

"But—"

"No, let me say it. I have to get it out while I can. Tim's a good guy. Our marriage wasn't bad, but it wasn't ever complete—because I couldn't have kids. He did his best to make me feel better about it. He swore that it didn't matter—but it did. I divorced him to set him free. And look what happened."

Audrey shook her head sadly.

"You don't need to feel sorry for me."

"I'm not feeling sorry for you! I'm kind of mad at you. You've always made out that Tim wanted to leave you, that he wanted kids more than he wanted you. He wasn't lying, Izzy. It really wasn't as important to him as being with you was. You decided what he wanted, and you pushed him away so that he could have it. Since he remarried and had his little girl, you've claimed that you were right—that that was what he wanted all along. It wasn't. It's what he went after when he couldn't have you anymore."

Izzy stared at her for a long moment. "He wanted a family."

"Yes, and so did you. But when you couldn't make it happen, he was happy for the two of you to build whatever life you could have. It was you that was so hung up on family being more important than anything else." Audrey gave her a stern look. "If you're going to tell me that you're holding back with Diego because you don't want to intrude on his family, I think I might throttle you!"

Izzy stared at her in surprise. "Why?"

"Ugh. Why can't you see it, Iz? Because families are what you make them. They're not exclusively reserved for the people you meet and marry when you're young and the children you have with them. I know you had it tough growing up, but it's like you somehow decided that because you didn't have a family, then you never get to be part of one. That's just not true, and I wish you'd see it. Look at Ted and me … we're making a new family with Ally and Brayden and Eddie and April. Do you think April's not part of it because she's not blood? Do you think that when Ally and Brayden meet someone, their partners will be left on the outside looking in?"

"No, but that's different."

"How? It's not different at all. You said yourself, Diego has Zack, they're just two guys, not a traditional family unit, but don't you think Maria is part of their family?"

"Of course, she is."

"Yes, she is because Zack loves her, and therefore, Diego does, too. And if you give them a chance, Zack and Maria will come to love you because Diego does. And if you let yourself, you'll grow to love them. That's how families work, Izzy. You choose each other, and you grow in love. A family is a group of people who choose to love each other and are loyal to each other. You're part of our family. You have been for years. Why can't you let yourself become a part of Diego's family? Let him become a part of yours?"

Izzy sat there, staring at her. "Are you done?"

Audrey nodded. "Sorry. It's just that it's frustrated me for years that you have this hang-up about family and about not being part of one when you're the only one who's ever put yourself on the outside. It cost you your marriage. It meant that you only ever got involved with unsuitable guys, and I don't want to see you let it ruin what you and Diego can have, okay?"

She nodded. "Okay. You made your point." She pursed her lips. "And you made it well. I can see what you're saying—"

"Hallelujah!"

She had to laugh at that. "Have you really tried to tell me this before?"

Audrey rolled her eyes. "Hundreds of times. But I'm not going to hold it against you that you refused to hear it before."

"Why's that?"

"Because if you had, you wouldn't be in this position with Diego now, and I honestly think he's the best thing that ever happened to you."

Izzy had to smile. "I think you could be right about that."

"Well, then don't screw it up! If I were you, I'd tell him how screwy you are about all this stuff and ask him to help you through it."

Izzy raised an eyebrow at her.

"Seriously. He's a grown man. He's not like Rafa or any of the other guys you've dated. If the two of you are going to make this work, you need to be able to talk to each other openly and honestly … about everything."

Izzy's heart was racing and not in a good way this time.

"What's your problem with talking to him about it?"

She had to think about it before she could answer. "I guess I have a problem with being vulnerable; it's just laying yourself open to getting hurt."

"That's one way of looking at it, but another way to see it is that it's trusting him to see who you really are, flaws and all … and to love you anyway."

"What if he doesn't?" That was the real fear. What if she admitted to him what a screw-up she really was, and it put him off her?

"I believe he will. He's not some kid looking for perfection. He's real. And he wants you to be real, too. You don't get to our age without taking some knocks and collecting some scars. I think it'll make him love you even more if you show him yours."

"But what if he doesn't?" she asked again.

"Then it wouldn't work out between you over the long term, and you're better off finding that out now."

Izzy turned and looked out at the lake. She knew Audrey was right. She should just talk to him and tell him why she was the way she was. She didn't like to think of herself as some weedy little female, though. Then again, she didn't think she liked big, confident, macho guys either, but once she'd relaxed and gone along with what was instead of how she thought things should be, she'd hadn't minded finding out that she was wrong!

~ ~ ~

Diego came out of the title office and slapped Austin on the back. "Thanks for all your help."

"It's been my pleasure. I'm sorry it took longer than I first expected."

"That was hardly your fault." Diego smiled as he realized that if they'd closed two weeks ago, he might not have gotten together with Izzy. "I believe everything works out at it should, in its own time."

Austin nodded. "I'd like to think that, too. What do you say, do you want to come over to the Boathouse for a drink to celebrate?"

"Thanks, but no. I want to get back over to the lodge at Four Mile and bring Izzy back to see the house."

"Oh. She's with you?"

Diego nodded.

"I'll let you get going then."

"Thanks. Will you be out tomorrow night? Zack said everyone's coming over here."

"I will. Though I'm not sure how long I'll stay."

Diego laughed. "When I was your age, I'd have shut the place down every weekend. You're young and single, why not make the most of it."

Diego recognized the look in his eye. "Ah. You don't wish to be single anymore? Who is she?"

Austin laughed. "What makes you think that?"

"I can tell. I've watched guys fall by the wayside over the years when they got hooked by a woman." He smiled. "Now, I've fallen, too. I can see it in your eyes. Do you want to tell me about it?"

For a moment, Austin looked as though he did. But then he shook his head. "No. You need to get back over to Four Mile, pick up your lady, and bring her back to see your new house. You've got a new life to get started on. You don't need to be hanging around here, listening to my woes. I appreciate the offer, though."

He was right. Diego couldn't wait to show Izzy the house. He hoped she was going to love it as much as he did. He grasped Austin's shoulder. "Promise me that if you need someone to talk to … someone older." He smiled. "I can't claim wiser, or even more experienced …"

Austin raised an eyebrow at that.

Diego chuckled. "In matters of the heart. If you're looking for something less complicated, then I'm your expert."

Austin laughed. "Thanks. I might take you up on the offer someday soon."

"You have my number. You know where I live. I'll help you any way I can, any time."

"Thanks. But for now, you need to get going. I'll no doubt see you around over the weekend."

Diego hurried back to the rental car. As he got in it, he realized that he should buy himself a car here now. Between Izzy's place and being up here at the lake, he spent more time in rental cars than in his own car these days. He smiled as he started the engine. Perhaps she'd let him buy her one, too—a matching set for the two of them.

His smile faded as he pulled out into the traffic on Main Street. First, he'd have to get her to admit that she loved him—that she wanted to be with him. Even then, she might not want him to buy her a car, but he'd stand more of a chance.

His phone rang as he turned onto East Shore Road, and he hit the button to answer. "Hello?"

"Hey." It was Ted.

"Hola, mi amigo."

Ted laughed. "You sound happy. I take it the closing went without a hitch?"

"It did. And when we get settled in, you'll be our first guests."

"Great. And you just answered my next question."

"Which was?"

"Whether you and Izzy are a we. She's good with it?"

"Hmm. I believe she will be. She's taking her time, and I'm respecting that."

"Wise man. Don't rush her."

"I won't. But what about you and Audrey? Your rushing things seems to have paid off."

Ted laughed. "In some respects, yes. But not in others. You're the one who now has a house here ready to move in."

"Yes, but only because you chose to build."

"True. I don't mind telling you that I'm a little envious that you get to sleep in your new house tonight. It'll be months before Audrey and I can do that."

"But it will be worth the wait. And you have a very nice rental home to wait in. If anything, I'm the one who's envious."

"Of what?"

"Of the fact you and Audrey are officially together. You might have to wait for your house to be ready, but you don't have to wait for her to be ready. She's wearing your ring. You get to sleep next to her every night, wake up beside her every morning."

"And you're ready for that with Izzy?"

"I am."

"But she's not?"

"No." He blew out a sigh. "She still has this thing that she's not really part of my life. I've told her, Ted ... told her that I love her. But I don't know if she doesn't believe me, or she just doesn't feel it. I asked her to come with me to the closing. She said she didn't want to be in the way. Why would she be in the way? I want her to spend time with Zack and Maria with me, but she doesn't want to intrude on family time. When it's just the two of us, I know everything's all right, but when it comes to living life ... building a life together, she backs out."

Ted didn't say anything.

"Are you still there? Are you seeing some problem that I'm missing?"

"I'm here."

"Tell me?"

Ted chuckled. "Who says I have anything to say about it?"

"Your silence does. Tell me ... do you think it's bad? Is it something I can get past?"

"I don't know, Diego. Obviously, I can't tell you what's going on with her; only she can do that. But my guess is that she doesn't fully trust you yet. And to be fair, why would she? It's only been a short time."

Diego sighed. "You're right."

"So, take your time. Go slow. Let her see that you're for real. Let her get to know Zack and Maria in her own time. I know you; you're full-on when you want something, and that might be scary to a woman like her."

"What do you mean, a woman like her?"

"Well, I don't want to say this the wrong way, but from what I understand, she hasn't been interested in long-term relationships for years, has she? When you first met her, you insisted that she wasn't interested in you because she prefers younger guys—guys she can push around is what you said. I'd guess that there's a reason she'd dated guys like that and avoided guys like you. You might want to figure out what that reason is and then do everything you can to reassure her that it's not a valid reason to stay away from you."

"What do you think her reason might be?" Diego's mind was racing now. Ted was right. He had spent every night with her for the last week. They'd been full-on since the moment Ted and Audrey had left them in Ventura. And somewhere along the way, he'd forgotten that she wasn't really into guys like him. Of course, he'd won her over, but how long would that last?

"I have no idea. That's something you need to talk to her about—not me or anyone else. I do know that when you go around trying to guess what's going on with a woman, you only tend to make things worse."

Diego chuckled at that. "I've heard guys say that before."

Ted laughed with him. "Because it's so true."

"I believe you. But it's not something I have experience with. For me, whenever it's gotten to the stage that something was going on with a woman that needed to be guessed at or figured out, I took that as my sign to move on."

"I know. That's how I know how serious you are about, Izzy. And it worries me a little."

"Why?"

"Because I hope, but I don't know, and I can't tell if she's as serious about you."

Diego frowned to himself as he drove. He hoped she was. He believed she might be. But if she were, why hadn't she told him that she loved him?

"Sorry. Say something? I don't mean to put a damper on things."

"It's all good. Of course, it worries me. But I have hope."

"She'd be nuts not to be serious about you. I mean, women always are."

Diego chuckled. "Of course. I am the great Diego Águila, all the women want me."

Ted laughed with him. "Exactly."

"Okay. I'll let you go. I'll call you tomorrow about coming over to see the house."

"I'd love to. But I know Izzy's your priority. Do whatever you need to get things right between the two of you. Audrey and I can come and see the house any time."

Diego made a face as he hung up. It made him sad that, unlike Ted and Audrey, he wasn't secure in the knowledge that he and Izzy could do things anytime. Because, unlike Ted with Audrey, he didn't know that she loved him, didn't know if she planned to be part of his life. He wanted to know. He needed to know. But no. What he needed to do was give her time to figure it out for herself. She'd tell him one way or another in her own good time. He got the feeling that pushing her for what he wanted would only push her away.

# Chapter Fifteen

"Wait there?"

Izzy nodded and watched Diego get out of the car. She looked up at the house and let out a low whistle. It was beautiful. It looked like a Tuscan manor, not something she might have expected to find in a small town like Summer Lake. There were some nice houses down by the water; she'd seen them when she and Audrey had taken a walk on their first visit here. But this place was in a league of its own.

She laughed when he came around and opened the door for her.

He took her arm when she got out. "What do you think?"

She nodded. "I can see why you fell in love with it. It's beautiful."

He winked at her. "I seem to be making a habit out of that, don't I?"

"Of what?"

"Of being so bowled over by beauty that I go and fall in love and have to have it."

She pursed her lips. He had to have it? That made her feel as though she was some prize he was pursuing because he had to win.

He winked at her and ducked his head to land a peck on her lips. "You can't deny that I've had you?"

She had to laugh. "No, I can't. Nor would I want to."

"And you won't deny that I get to have you again later? That we can christen our new bed?"

She searched his face. He kept talking about this place as *ours*.

His smile was cocky as he looked back at her, but his eyes were as serious as she'd ever seen them. "Please don't deny me?"

She shook her head. When he looked at her like that, she doubted that she'd ever be able to deny him anything. Not that he needed to know that.

He took her hand and led her up the steps to the front door. While he unlocked it, she turned to look out at the grounds. The rental car sat on the circular driveway. It was quite a place.

"Are you ready?" She turned back to him, and he put his hands on her shoulders and looked down into her eyes.

"Are you ready for this?" he asked again.

She laughed. "You make it sound as though we're about to enter some magical wonderland."

He dropped a kiss on her lips and nodded enthusiastically. "That's because we are, Miss Isobel. But only if you're ready."

She looped her arms up around his neck and pressed herself against him as she kissed him. She didn't know what to do with the serious expression in his eyes, and she wasn't sure she wanted to try to figure out what he meant. But she knew that she could distract him with a magical adventure in the bedroom if he'd take her there.

She got lost in his kiss, and she knew she was on the right track when she felt him pressing into her belly. God, he felt so good. She couldn't wait to explore the bedroom.

He lifted his head and smiled down at her, then he hooked one arm behind her legs and scooped her up off her feet.

She gasped and closed her arms around his neck in surprise. "What are you …"

The question dried up in her throat as he looked up at the doorway and took a step toward it. "Are you ready?" he asked again.

Her heart felt as though it might beat out of her chest. He was asking if he could carry her across the threshold? That was what people did when they got married! He wasn't asking … He couldn't be …

He met her gaze, and his eyes bored into hers. He didn't ask again, just raised an eyebrow.

She tightened her grip around his neck. What was she afraid of? What had Audrey said? That he was the best thing that had ever happened to her. That was it. And she was right. Why on earth would she ever want to say no to this big, gorgeous man? She smiled and nodded.

She'd half expected him to look as though he'd won some battle, some duel they were engaged in. Instead, there was no denying the relief that mixed with happiness as he strode inside and closed the door behind them with his foot.

He dropped his head and landed a kiss on her lips. "Thank you."

She chuckled. "I think I'm the one who should be thanking you."

"We can fight about that later. But first, you need to see the house, and we need to christen our bed."

"I think you've got that in the wrong order."

He raised an eyebrow at her, and she smiled. "The house isn't going anywhere. This moment won't ever come again."

His expression softened, and he nodded and turned toward the stairs. She wriggled to get down, but he tightened his grip on her. "Just this once?" he asked with a smile. "I'm not getting any younger. I may never be able to carry you up the stairs to our bed again."

She nodded happily. If he could manage it, she wasn't going to argue.

He carried her up the stairs and into the master bedroom. It was a beautiful room, with huge windows looking out on the lake. Sparkling reflections danced on the ceiling as he lay her down on the bed.

~ ~ ~

As Diego set her down, his heart buzzed in his chest. He felt like he'd finally found the place he was supposed to be in the world—and the woman he was supposed to be with.

She looked up into his eyes and opened her mouth to speak. She looked as if she was about to make a joke, but then stopped, and her face grew serious.

"You really mean this, don't you?"

He nodded and lay down beside her. "I mean this more than I've ever meant anything in my life, Izzy. I don't want to say too much because I don't know if you're ready to hear it."

She shook her head slightly, and his smile faded.

"Don't say it."

He started to speak, but she put a finger to his lips. "Don't tell me; show me."

He put his arm around her and drew her closer to him. Showing her was something that he knew he could do. He propped himself up on one elbow and drew her under him as he brushed his lips over hers. Her arms came up around his back, and she clung to him as he kissed her deeply. There was something about the way she kissed him. She didn't just yield to him, as so many women had. She was assertive. She opened up to him, but she expected him to do the same. She demanded that he let her in.

His hands roved over her returning as they so often did to her full breasts. Her hands closed around his ass and rocked him against her. She felt so good underneath him, but his pants were now tight, restricting him, keeping him from her. Whether she read his thoughts or felt the same way, she unfastened his belt and slid her hand inside his shorts, closing her fingers around him.

Within seconds their clothes lay in a pile on the floor, and he looked down at her beautiful naked breasts. She laughed and slapped his arm. "Hey, I'm up here."

He trailed his fingers over her nipple as he looked up at her with a smile. "Oh. Hello. It's nice to see you."

She half chuckled, half moaned as he rolled the taut peak between his finger and thumb. "Are you saying you don't like all the attention I pay to the ladies?"

"No," she breathed.

"Would you rather I stop?" He took his hand away, and she opened her eyes.

Her next words made him even harder than he had been.

"Please don't stop. Don't ever stop."

His hand returned to its work. He wanted to ask if she meant that—don't *ever* stop. But he didn't dare. He didn't want to kill the moment by asking for more than she was ready to give.

Her hands were around his ass again. He walked his fingers down over her ribcage, on down over her stomach, and she moaned that moan he'd grown to love when he slid his hand between her legs.

She rocked her hips in time with him as he stroked her. She was so beautiful, her cheeks and neck flushed with desire for him.

"Please?" she breathed.

He smiled. "Patience, Miss Isobel. We're just getting started." He dipped a finger inside her, loving how hot and wet she was for him.

She shook her head. "Please, Diego. I want you." She moved away from his hand and wriggled herself underneath him. "Don't tease me. Make love to me."

He cocked his head to one said. She'd said many things to him in bed, some of them had surprised him even while they turned him on. He hadn't expected her to be so direct. But this was the first time she'd called it making love.

He curled his arm around her and drew her under him. If that was what she wanted, who was he to deny her? He dropped his head and nuzzled his lips against her neck. Her arms came up around him, and she spread her legs wider so that he was pushing into her heat.

He had to force himself to go slowly at first. His hips wanted to thrust hard, to drive himself home deep inside her, but she was asking for tenderness, and he planned to give it to her. She bit down on his shoulder when he entered her. Her

162

SJ McCoy

legs came up around his, and he drove deeper. Something about the feel of her feet on his calves drove him wild. She bucked her hips underneath him and he moved with her. The slow beginning gave way to a frantic rhythm as he buried himself deep over and over again. She felt so good, closing around him, welcoming him home. That was how it felt. She was home to him now.

She was carrying him away, and there was nothing he could do but to go with her. Their bodies moved together frantically in the rhythm that had become theirs. They carried each other higher and higher until he felt her tense, and she screamed, "Diego!"

That took him over the edge. Her orgasm triggered his, and he found his release deep inside her. She kept moaning his name over and over again. He felt as though he was losing himself inside her. "Izzy!" he gasped as waves of pleasure crashed through him and into her.

When they finally lay still, he rested his head on her shoulder. She turned to meet his gaze and kissed his cheek. There was a tenderness in her eyes he hadn't seen before. Something about this time was different. He knew it. She'd been vocal from their first time, but up until now, she screamed, *yes*, or *oh, God!* But this time, this time she'd cried his name. That felt different, and when she spoke, he understood why.

"I love you, Diego."

His heart felt as if it might burst in his chest. He claimed her mouth in a kiss that had her rocking again underneath him as the aftershocks rolled through them.

He lifted his head and smiled down at her. "I love you, Izzy. Say it again?"

Her eyes shone as she laughed. "I love you."

He tangled his fingers in her hair. "And I love you." He held her gaze for a long moment. "Does that mean everything is possible now?"

She nodded slowly. "Perhaps not right now, but with time."

He dropped a kiss on the tip of her nose. "For you, *mi amor*, I have all the time in the world."

~ ~ ~

Izzy sipped her drink and looked out at the lake. It shimmered crimson and gold in the last of the afternoon sun. It was beautiful out here on the terrace. She looked up at the house. The whole place was beautiful. And Diego wanted her to live here with him? She shook her head in wonder.

"No, what?" he asked as he came back out to join her.

"Huh?"

"You were shaking your head at something."

"I was shaking my head in wonder."

"About?" He raised an eyebrow and smirked at her. "About how good we are in bed together?"

She laughed. "Not at that no, but I'm not denying that we are."

"Good." He dropped a kiss on her lips before he sat down. "Want to tell me what?"

She nodded slowly. "I should. I'm finding it hard to take all this in. You … this house …" She shrugged.

"The fact that I want you to move up here with me?"

She nodded.

"Is there any part of you that doesn't want to?"

"No …"

"But?"

"I feel like there should be at least a part of me that doesn't, you know?"

"I don't. Why should there be?"

"Apart from all the obvious reasons? Like it's too soon. We haven't known each other that long. I'd be moving into your house." She blew out a sigh.

"Yes. Apart from all of that." He held her gaze. "We can overcome all of those. You know we can."

She had to smile. His confidence used to piss her off. Now, she understood it. He was only being honest. "I do."

He waggled his eyebrows at that, but she didn't want to go near it. "So, tell me about this part of you that you think should resist—shouldn't want to move in here with me."

She shrugged. "I shouldn't want to give up my independence."

"Who says you have to?"

"I would be, though. I'd be living in your house."

"Our house."

She made a face at him. "You can call it that all you like, but it's yours."

"Over time, I hope that you'll come to see it as ours. I want you to come to see everything as ours. And you know what that means, even if I'm not allowed to say it yet."

She nodded.

"And it's not even because it's too soon, is it? That's not your reason for thinking you should hold back."

"Okay, if you're so smart, you tell me what my problem is?"

He gave her a wry smile. "I'm not *that* smart, but I believe that what's holding you back from going all-in with me is about what happened in your past rather than what might happen in our future."

She held his gaze for a long moment until she finally looked away. Of course, he was right.

"You don't have to tell me until you're ready. You don't ever have to tell me if you don't want to."

She reached across the table and took hold of his hand. "You're such a sweetheart."

He swaggered his shoulders. "Finally, you're starting to understand me."

She laughed. "Don't spoil it. I was about to tell you."

He looked serious now. "Only if you want to."

"I do. I don't talk about my past much, but if we're going to do this ... if we're taking a shot at being together for real, then you need to know." She stared out at the lake again. "I don't know where to start."

"Do you want to tell me about your family?"

Her head snapped around, and she met his gaze. "I don't have one."

He squeezed her hand. "You do now. You have me. But I mean, tell me about your childhood, your people?"

She blew out a sigh. She knew what he meant. "Okay. I don't know who my people are. I was in the foster system from when I was a little kid. I was moved around a lot."

His big brown eyes looked so sad. She had to swallow before she went on.

"Don't feel sorry for me, okay? I can't deal with that."

He nodded. "So, you never settled with a family?"

"I did. They found me a placement when I was fourteen." She closed her eyes. "I stayed with them till I aged out."

He raised an eyebrow. "Aged out?"

"When you get to eighteen, you're on your own. I was lucky, I got a place at the local community college and shared an apartment with some friends."

"But you didn't keep in touch with the family?"

She shuddered. "No. It was a relief to get away from them."

His eyebrows knit together. "Why?"

She looked out at the lake for a few minutes before she could continue. "Because the father, the ..." Seeing the look on his face, it was obvious that he knew what she was about to say. "He was a big guy. A real man's man. You know?"

Diego nodded grimly. "I think I do."

She shrugged. "It started not long after I first went to them. He told me it was just how things worked. That I needed to show him how grateful I was." She sucked in a deep breath and let it out slowly. "I'm over it. I've dealt with it. I went through years of therapy." She gave him a smile that she knew wouldn't convince him of anything. "I'm healed. I'm well-adjusted. I survived, and I moved on."

He tugged on her hand and jerked his head for her to come to him. It felt like the most natural thing in the world to go to him and to sit in his lap, to let him close his arms around her and hold her close to his chest.

It surprised her to feel tears on her face. She hadn't cried over it in years. It truly was behind her.

He tucked his fingers under her chin and made her look up at him. It blew her away to see tears rolling down his cheeks, too.

"It breaks my heart, Izzy."

She shook her head. "No. It is what it is. Please, whatever you do, don't go feeling sorry for me. That'd kill what we have faster than anything."

He brushed his sleeve over his eyes and nodded. "Okay. I can understand that. You don't need my pity. You deserve my respect and my admiration … and you have them." He planted a kiss on her lips. "And you have my heart and my love."

She wrapped her arms around his neck and rested her wet cheek against his. "And just so you know for sure, you have mine, too."

He nodded. "But I'm the last guy you wanted to fall for?"

"Yup."

"And now I understand why."

"I hope so."

His arms tightened around her. "You know I would never ask anything of you that you don't want to give?"

"Of course, I do. I wouldn't be here if I didn't know that."

"And all of that is the reason that you avoided men like me, why you stuck with little boys you could push around?"

She had to smile at that. "They weren't exactly little boys."

"No, but you know what I mean. Younger and not so …" He smiled. "Like you used to think of me—full of themselves."

She laughed. "I still think that of you. You are full of yourself. I just don't call you out on it so much now, because I understand that you have reason to be."

He chuckled at that. It was a low, deep sound that rumbled up through his chest. "I have even more reason to be now, too."

"Oh, yeah? Why's that?"

"Because the most beautiful woman I ever met told me today that she loves me."

She nodded.

"And I love her, with all my heart and soul. And I plan to keep her safe and make her happy ... until the day she dies."

She looked into his eyes, and he nodded.

"I can't take away what happened in the first part of your life, Izzy, but I intend to make sure that the rest of your life is happy and filled with love ... if you'll let me?"

Tears started to roll down her cheeks again, and when he kissed her, she could feel them mix with his.

# Chapter Sixteen

Diego looked around the kitchen. He'd told Izzy the same as he'd told Zack and Maria: that this afternoon was no big deal. The two of them were coming over to see the house. That was all. Of course, this would be the first time that they got to see him and Izzy together, officially, as a couple. He didn't do nervous, but he was eager for the afternoon to go well.

Izzy had gone to meet up with Audrey this morning. He was glad that she had her friend here. And from what Ted had told him, Audrey and her kids were going to do everything that they could to persuade her to stay.

He knew that they saw her as part of their family. They'd want her here with them even if it weren't for him. He closed his eyes and clenched his fists as he thought about what she'd told him last night. It made his blood boil. He wanted to hunt the bastard down and kill him. He sucked in a deep breath and let it out slowly. And Izzy wouldn't be happy if she knew that he felt that way. She was her own person. She'd told him because she trusted him. She wasn't looking for his sympathy or his help in any way. She'd only told him because it helped him to understand why she was the way she was.

He started when the oven timer dinged. He'd kept himself busy by preparing snacks for when Zack and Maria came. He pulled a tray of empanadas out and set them on the counter. Zack had always loved them.

His phone rang, and he picked it up. He didn't recognize the number and almost let it go to voicemail. He made a face and swiped to answer.

"Hello?"

"Diego?"

He frowned, the voice sounded familiar, but he couldn't place it. "Yes?"

"It's me, Manny!"

He laughed. "Manny?! How are you? Where are you? It's great to hear from you."

"I'm doing well, thanks. I'm still in Sacramento, but I won't be for much longer."

"No? Why's that?"

"I'm taking early retirement."

"What? You're way too young to retire! What will you do with yourself?"

Manny laughed. "I want to retire while I'm still young enough to do something with what's left of my life. As a matter of fact, that's what I'm calling you about."

"What?"

"I'll be visiting Summer Lake next month, and I talked to Zack."

Diego frowned. "About Morales?"

"No! You don't need to worry about him anymore. They threw away the key."

"That's good to know, but I'm still wary that he might somehow come around again."

"It's not going to happen. And that isn't what I called Zack about anyway. When I was up at Summer Lake with him— when all that went down—I took a liking to the place. And now that I'm coming up on retirement, I'm looking for somewhere quiet and peaceful—"

Diego grinned. "And Summer Lake fits the bill perfectly!"

Manny laughed. "It might do. I have a couple of options I want to explore. I'm going to Hope Falls this weekend."

"Yeah, that's a nice place. But you need to come to Summer Lake. Did Zack tell you that I just bought a house here?"

"He did. That's why I'm calling. You being there might just swing the decision for me. I'd like to think that wherever I move, I'm going to know at least a couple of people. I know some guys in Hope Falls, but they're that much younger. I thought it'd be the same at Summer Lake; I know Zack and Colt, but if you're going to be there …"

Diego laughed. "You won't be the only old fart? You'll have me, and Ted's building a place here, too."

"He is? Zack didn't mention that. To be fair, he didn't get the chance. I was too busy interrogating him about your reasons to move there."

Diego smiled through pursed lips. He knew the way Manny worked. He wouldn't ask the question directly; he'd wait for Diego to fill in the blanks for him.

After a few moments of silence, Manny laughed. "You're not going to tell me unless I ask, are you?"

"I am not. Your FBI interrogation tactics won't work on me. I'm not going to incriminate myself."

"There's something incriminating?"

Diego laughed. "No, but you're going to have a lot more questions when I tell you."

"It's okay. Zack told me there's a woman."

"She's not just a woman, Manny."

"No?"

"No. She's … she's …" He didn't know how to say it. Then he laughed. He did know how to say it; he just didn't know how Manny would react. "She's the one. I'm in love."

"No shit?!"

He had to laugh. "No shit. You have to come up here. You have to meet her. You'll understand."

"I can't wait. Now I'm even more eager to visit. You're serious?"

"I am. Whenever you want to come, you let me know. You can stay here."

"No. Thanks, but I'll rent a place. I want to find my feet— see how living there feels. If it's something I'd enjoy, you know? I can't figure that out if I'm staying with you as your guest."

"True. Do you know when you'll be here?"

"It'll be next month."

"And how long will you stay? Have you done anything about renting a place?"

"Not yet. I don't suppose you know anyone, do you? There are a couple of property management agencies online, but …"

"As a matter of fact, I do. The agent I used to buy this place is a great guy. Austin. I'll send you his contact details when we get off the phone."

"That's great, thanks. I need to get going, anyway."

"Okay. I'll email you now. And keep in touch. Let me know when you're going to be here."

"Will do. It's good to talk to you."

"You, too."

Diego hung up with a smile. Manny had been a good friend to him and Zack over the years. If he were to move here to Summer Lake, it'd make Diego happy.

He checked his watch. Izzy should be back soon, and Zack and Maria wouldn't be too far behind her.

~ ~ ~

Izzy walked back across the parking lot to the rental car. She felt a little guilty that Diego had insisted that she should use the car. She'd suggested that she rent a second one, but he'd said there was no point. He wasn't going anywhere this morning, and even if he needed to, he could easily walk into town from the house. He was right. And at least he hadn't said that he'd rent one for her. She'd braced herself against that. He might be loaded, but she wasn't exactly a pauper; she could pay her own way.

"Izzy?"

She turned when she heard her name being called. She didn't see anyone she recognized.

A pretty girl with long dark hair waved at her. "Hi, Izzy!"

She frowned. She still wasn't sure who it was.

The girl hurried over and greeted her with a smile. "Sorry. I know who you are, but you don't know me! I'm Maria. Zack's girlfriend ... fiancée."

"Oh! Hi. It's nice to meet you." She held out her hand, but Maria looked at it and then wrapped her in a hug.

"Sorry. I can't help it! I'm so excited to meet you. I thought I was running late. Zack texted me to say I need to get home so we can get over to your place. But if you're still here, I guess I'm okay, too."

Izzy liked her immediately. She laughed. "Either that or we're both late." She checked her watch. "I thought I'd be back at the house by now, but Audrey and I got to talking, and you know how that goes."

"I do. I did the same thing with Angel and Roxy." She slipped her arm through Izzy's and started walking. "Where are you parked?"

"I'm over there." She pointed to the end of the row.

"I'm down there, too." Maria smiled at her. "Please tell me you're as happy as Diego is?"

Izzy stared at her for a moment.

"Sorry! I can't help it. He's so wonderful. I just love him to pieces, and Zack does, too. We want to see him happy, and you've made him so very happy." She stopped. "You should probably ignore me. I'm gushing on about Diego. I don't mean to put you under any pressure or anything."

Izzy had to smile. "It's okay. It doesn't feel like pressure. And I don't mind telling you that he's made me happy, too. You're right. He's a wonderful man."

Maria grinned. "So, you're going to move here with him?"

"I haven't wrapped my head around that yet."

"Oh." Maria looked so disappointed that Izzy felt bad.

"I'm not saying I won't. But he and I have a lot more to figure out first." She smiled. "And you seem like a real sweetheart, but—"

"Of course! Forgive me. I shouldn't even be asking. It's none of my business. Except it feels like my business. I mean, he's Zack's dad, and we so want him to decide to stay up here. It seems like the only reason he wouldn't stay now is if you …" She stopped short. "Listen to me! Just ignore me, okay? Let's go all the way back to hello, and I'll say I'm Maria, it's nice to meet you."

Izzy laughed. "And I'm Izzy; it's nice to meet you, too." They'd reached the car now. "I'll see you at the house in a little while. I'm glad we did this first."

"Are you? I feel like I just put my foot in it big time."

"No. You're fine. You care about him. That's understandable. You're family, after all."

Maria nodded happily. "And I get the feeling that soon you will be, too." She gave Izzy another hug. "We're going to have to stick together you and me. We have ourselves two very strong-willed men."

Izzy smiled at her. "You don't strike me as a meek little thing."

Maria laughed. "Nope. Not at all."

"Perhaps it's them who need to worry about two strong-willed women, then?"

Maria shook her head. "Zack doesn't worry about that. He loves me for it." She smiled. "And I get the impression that his dad's the same way with you."

Izzy got into the car and started it up. She dialed Diego's number. She should call and let him know she was on the way. She waved at Maria when she pulled out.

"*Hola, mi amor.*"

A little shiver ran down her spine at the sound of his voice. "I love it when you talk dirty to me."

He laughed. "I don't think calling you my love is dirty, is it?"

"No. It's just the way it sounds, not the words you say."

"Hmm. Perhaps I need to talk to you some more later?"

"Yes, you do. Talk to me like that, and I'm all yours."

"In that case, I will. I'll talk to you like that just as soon as you get home."

"I'll be there as soon as I can. I'm just leaving the lodge now. Sorry I ran late."

"There's no need to apologize."

"I know, but you're stuck at home, and …"

"It's all good. I'm not stuck here. I'm happy here. And it doesn't matter if Zack and Maria get here before you."

"They won't. I just ran into Maria. She's leaving here now, too. And she's going home to get Zack before they come to the house."

"Okay. Then I'll get you to myself for a few minutes before they arrive."

She smiled at that. She was looking forward to getting to know Maria and Zack better. But she loved the idea of a little time alone with him first.

~ ~ ~

Diego smiled when he saw Zack's truck pull up in front of the house. "They're here."

He loved the way Izzy straightened up her shoulders. She came across so strong as if nothing fazed her, but he knew better now. She just put on a brave face. She was strong; he'd hadn't been mistaken about that. Stronger than any woman he'd ever known. But she wasn't as indifferent as she made out. She was nervous about meeting his son. But that wasn't any sign of weakness—not in his eyes. It only made him love her more. She was nervous because she knew how much his son meant to him.

He went to her and put his arm around her shoulders. "He's a good boy ... well, he's not a boy anymore. He's a fine young man. I think you'll like him."

The look in her eyes slayed him. "I'm not worried about me liking him. I'm worried about him liking me."

"He'll love you! Just like his papá does." He dropped a kiss on her lips.

"He shouldn't. Not at first, at least. He needs to get to know me and to make his own judgment. You need to look at this from his point of view. To him, I'm just some woman who's come along and gotten her claws into his dad. He has every right to be cautious."

Diego shook his head with a smile. "He trusts me. He knows I wouldn't have fallen in love with just some woman." He kissed her again. "And I do love you, Miss Isobel."

He felt her relax, and she smiled. "And I love you. I don't know what you did to me, but you made me fall in love with you."

"And that's all that matters. It's all Zack needs to know." The doorbell rang, and he walked her to the door. He opened it and smiled. "Welcome, welcome. Come on in."

Zack grinned at him. "I love this place!"

"So do we."

Zack turned to Izzy. "Sorry. It's great to see you again. How are you?"

Diego smiled at Maria as Zack wrapped Izzy in a hug. She looked a little taken aback at first, but she relaxed and hugged him back. "I'm good, thanks. It's great to see you, too."

Maria elbowed Zack out of the way with a laugh. "Move over. I need a hug, too." She grinned at Izzy. "I haven't seen you for ages!"

Izzy laughed. "You're right, it must've been at least an hour."

"Come on in." Diego smiled at them. "Do you want a drink, or do you want the tour first?"

"The tour!" said Maria.

"A drink," said Zack.

Diego looked at Izzy. "Do you want to be bartender or tour guide?"

She laughed. "I think I'd make a better bartender."

Diego watched Zack follow her into the kitchen. He'd hoped that they would get a few minutes alone together. It was important to him that they should not only get along but hopefully build some kind of friendship of their own.

Maria winked at him. "They'll be fine. She's awesome."

He winked back at her. "Is it strange that I'm nervous?"

She shook her head rapidly. "I get it. But I don't think you have anything to worry about." She slipped her arm through his. "Come on. I wasn't joking that I want the grand tour."

He led her through to the family room with its big picture windows overlooking the shoreline.

~ ~ ~

"What would you like?" asked Izzy. Zack seemed nice enough, but she wouldn't blame him if he was suspicious of her or her motives.

He smiled. "Honestly?"

She raised an eyebrow at him, wondering what was coming.

He laughed. "I'd like you to relax! I promise I don't bite."

"Oh."

His smile was a lot like his dad's. "I just want to get to know you. I want you to get to know us. You make my dad happy, so I'm inclined to think you must be pretty awesome."

She had to smile. "Well, that's a relief. I thought you were maybe seeing me as some gold-digger who had her claws in him."

He laughed out loud at that. "The thought never even crossed my mind. Think about it. Dad's had to run off his fair share of gold-diggers over the years. He can spot them a mile off."

Izzy nodded. It hadn't occurred to her before, but of course, he would have had plenty of experience with women who saw him as a potential meal ticket.

"Sorry." Zack looked serious now. "That probably sounded wrong."

She shrugged. "It sounded like what it was—the truth. And don't worry. It's not as though you're all of a sudden making me realize that I'm not the first woman to come into his life." She had to laugh. "And I'm not going to pretend that he's the first man to come into mine. I suppose we're very similar when you think about it. We've both seen relationships as short and sweet in the past." She hoped that conveyed what she meant without making her sound bad. "Neither of us were into anything serious. It just kind of … kind of …" She searched for the right words. "Well, I don't know about your dad, but for me, it came out of the blue. I don't mind telling you that I thought he was full of it when I first met him."

Zack laughed. "I hope you told him so?"

She laughed with him. "I did. On several occasions, but he didn't give up." She smiled. "And with time, I've come to realize that he's not full of it. He's …" She met Zack's gaze. "He's pretty awesome, isn't he?"

Zack nodded happily. "I think he is."

"Okay." She pulled herself together. "Now we've got that out of the way, what do you want to drink?"

"I'll take a soda, please."

Izzy hesitated as she opened the fridge. She almost felt as though he should be getting it, and she should be sitting back as the visitor, the guest.

Just like his dad, he seemed to read her mind. "I'm going to say one more thing because I get the impression that you need to hear it. I'm glad that he's met you. I know he wants this to be your home—the both of you. And if there's anything I can do—and Maria, she loves you already—if there's anything we can ever do to help, to make this feel like home or anything else, please say so. I want to see him happy. It's obvious that you make him happy."

She turned back to him and set the soda down on the counter. "Thanks, Zack. He makes me happy. I want to make this work. I don't know what I'm doing ... how to handle it, but I'll get there."

He put his hand on top of hers. "You will. And like I say, if there's anything you need help with—if ever you want to talk—I'm here for you. We're going to be family, after all."

She had to swallow around a lump in her throat. "And you don't mind that?"

He frowned. "Mind? Why would I mind?" He squeezed her hand. "I love the idea. I just don't want anything to scare you off."

Wow. And she'd been expecting him to maybe give her a hard time.

Diego appeared in the doorway with Maria at his side. He looked at the way Zack's hand rested on top of hers, and then he smiled—first at Zack, then at her. He didn't say anything as he came into the kitchen, but that smile said it all.

# Chapter Seventeen

"What do you think?" asked Izzy as she came down the stairs.

Diego rubbed his hands together with a grin and went to meet her. "I think we just had a change of plan."

She gave him a puzzled look, and he had to laugh. He cupped her breast in his hand and landed a kiss on her lips. "Looking like that, Miss Isobel, the only place I want to take you is back upstairs."

She laughed and swatted his hand away. "There'll be plenty of time for that when we get home."

His heart buzzed in his chest.

"What? What's that look on your face about? I mean it. I want to go. We said we'd see Zack and Maria and Audrey and Ted."

He nodded. "And we will. This look on my face isn't about that. It's because you just called this place home." He closed his arms around her and looked down into her eyes. "Please tell me that you want it to be our home?"

She nodded. "I do. I can't just snap my fingers and say okay, this is it now. But I can tell you that I love the idea. And ..."

She smiled. "I can also tell you that Zack and Maria make it easy to feel as though we could all become ... you know."

"Family?"

She nodded again. "Stop grinning at me like that. I'm getting there, okay? But it'll come more easily by letting it happen than it will by constantly talking about it."

He dropped a kiss on the tip of her nose. "Then, I won't say another word ... for now."

"Thank you. And going back to the original question, keep your hands to yourself, and tell me if this outfit is okay?"

He smiled through pursed lips and shook his head.

"No? Why? What's wrong? Is it too dressy for the Boathouse?"

He nodded, still trying to hide his smile. "It's far too dressy."

"How?"

He chuckled. "Your girls are all covered up, and from the way they're pointing at me, they'd rather be free in the fresh air."

She laughed and slapped his arm. "Are you saying I need to wear something more modest?"

"No! I'm saying I'd rather you weren't wearing anything at all. But ..." He blew out an exaggerated sigh. "If you insist that we have to go out, then that outfit is perfect. You look amazing, but then you always do."

She rolled her eyes. "You don't need to keep feeding me lines, you know. I'm a sure thing."

He laughed. "They're not lines. You should know better than this by now."

Her smile was much softer when she looked up at him. "I do know, but we can still play, can't we?"

He slid his hand down over her ass and squeezed. "That's what I want to do—play with you—but you insist that we must go out instead."

She swatted at his hand again with a laugh. "And I also told you that there'll be plenty of time for that when we come home."

"Home." He nodded happily.

He squeezed her hand as they walked down Main Street toward the resort, and she looked up at him. "Can you see yourself feeling at home in this town as well as in our house?"

"I can. In fact, I kind of already do. It's a great little place, and everyone's so friendly. All my favorite people in the world are already here."

"Mine, too. But I need you to know that you're my most favorite person of all. What matters to me now is being where you are."

He loved the way she smiled. She was starting to relax, not just with him, but with the reality of where they were going. "I want to be where you are, too."

"Do you want to just stay here then?"

She pursed her lips. "I guess we could. I'd need to go home and get more clothes and get my things for work, but … yeah … I'd like to stay."

He grinned. This was going better than he'd dared to hope. "Very well, then. We can go back on Monday or Tuesday. I'll drop you at home while I go back to Laguna. I need to go to the office and stop by my house, too. I need to get more clothes and make sure Carmen is going to be okay if I'm not back for a while."

He felt her tense and had to wonder what he'd said wrong.

"What is it?"

She frowned. "I don't want this to sound how it's going to sound. I don't want to feel the way this feels ... but who the hell is Carmen?"

He had to laugh. "I'm so sorry. Carmen is my housekeeper. She's been with me for over twenty-five years. She's wonderful. You'll love her."

"Oh." She didn't look as relieved as he'd hoped she would with that explanation.

"Don't think I'm a lazy, no-good man who can't take care of myself. That's not the reason she stays with me."

"What is then?"

He shrugged. "She's good people. It's a good job for her."

"So, you hired her out of the goodness of your heart?"

"No. I hired her because I needed someone to watch Zack when his mother left us." He didn't know how this would sound to Izzy, but he needed her to understand. "She started out as a babysitter. When I became more successful, she moved in as a full-time housekeeper. After Zack left home, I kept her on because ... well, because she'd become part of the family. And the rest of her family depends on her income."

Izzy smiled. "Sorry. That's wonderful. You're wonderful. I didn't mean to be critical. You just gave me a shock. I've never heard about her before."

"I'm sorry. She's been on vacation for the last few weeks. She's been helping her daughter with the new baby."

Izzy nodded.

He smiled at her. "Were you jealous?"

"No!" Her eyes flashed as she denied it. But then she pursed her lips. "Okay, I'll admit it. Yes, I was. I just wondered who this woman was who you needed to check was okay before you move in with me."

He put his arm around her shoulders. "And now you know. She's someone I feel responsible for, not someone I need to check in with. And hope you also know that there isn't anyone you need to feel jealous about. There never will be." He landed a kiss on her lips. "I love you, Izzy. You've stolen my heart."

She smiled up at him. "You've stolen mine, too."

"And I don't plan to give it back."

It was already busy when they got to the Boathouse. Izzy smiled as she let Diego forge them a path through the crowd to get to the bar. It reminded her of the first night they'd met. She noticed how people got out of his way to let them pass then. Powerful. She shook her head. That was how she'd seen him. And it was kind of how he was, but not in an overbearing way.

He turned and looked back at her. "Are you okay?"

She smiled and squeezed his hand. "I'm great." She was, too. She didn't resent him taking the lead. She didn't feel as though he was treating her like the *little woman*. He was just being who he was. And she loved who he was.

When they finally made it to the bar, he put his arm around her shoulders and dropped a kiss on her lips. "Champagne?"

She raised an eyebrow at him.

"It's what we drank the night we met."

She laughed. So, he'd been remembering that night, too? "Sure."

Kenzie, the bartender, got finished serving the guy beside them. "What can I get you, sugar?" she asked before she even looked up. When she did, it was obvious that she recognized Diego. "Oh, hey, gorgeous! It's good to see you." She turned and looked at Izzy. "Oh! And you, too!" She grinned. "I didn't know the two of you were an item."

Diego tightened his arm around Izzy's shoulders. "Neither did Miss Isobel the last time we were here."

She laughed and shook her head at Kenzie. "Ignore him. He's full of himself."

Kenzie laughed with her. "He is. But he has reason to be. There are going to be a lot of disappointed ladies around here. You snagged yourself a hot item, girlfriend."

Diego looked a little wary. Was he worried that she might feel insecure? She raised an eyebrow at him. "Nah. He's the lucky one, and he knows it."

Diego and Kenzie both laughed at that, and Kenzie high-fived her across the bar. "That's what I like to see, a woman who knows her worth." She looked at Diego. "I hope you know what you've got."

He dropped a kiss on Izzy's lips. "I do. And I don't plan to let her go."

"Aww. You guys are too cute. What can I get you, though? We're slammed, and much as I'd like to stay and chat, I need to keep moving."

"A bottle of Veuve Clicquot Grand Dame," said Diego.

Kenzie grinned at him. "Coming right up."

"You remembered," said Izzy.

"Of course, I did."

She smiled. "We were celebrating Audrey's new beginning that night. She was just starting to get right with herself. We didn't know that she was about to meet Ted."

He looked into her eyes. "You didn't know you were about to meet me, either."

"No. But it seems like the champagne did."

He raised an eyebrow.

"We were laughing about their slogan—let life surprise you. I know life took Audrey by surprise that night in the form of Ted. But damn if you haven't surprised me even more."

He grinned. "You don't think you've surprised me? You don't think I'm surprised at myself? In fifty-seven years on this earth, no woman has affected me the way you have." He took hold of her hand and brought it to his lips. He brushed them over the inside of her wrist and sent shivers chasing each other down her spine.

She looked up into his eyes. "That still has the same effect on me as the first time you did it."

His eyes shone with amusement. "But now you believe that I mean it—that it's not just some move."

She nodded. "I do."

Kenzie set a bottle and two flutes down on the bar. "Here you go, guys. Enjoy." She looked at Diego. "On your tab?"

"Thanks, Kenzie."

Izzy looked around. "Do you want to stay here or go and see who we can find?"

He gave her the glasses while he got the bottle and took hold of her hand.

She let him lead her outside onto the deck. It was much quieter out here. The band would be playing later, but for now, just a few people were sitting at the tables.

He led her to a picnic bench right at the edge of the deck, by the rail overlooking the water. She watched as he opened the bottle. She'd been right about him on that first night. He was one of those guys who just did everything well, made everything look easy. He grinned as he filled the flutes and handed one to her.

"What?" she asked. "I know you. You're looking far too pleased with yourself. What are you up to?"

He tried to look innocent, but he didn't pull it off. "I'm not up to anything. But I do want to ask you to drink a toast with me."

She raised an eyebrow.

"That first night, I asked you to drink to new beginnings with me, but you refused."

She nodded. "I compromised with you, though. I drank to new friends."

He ran his hand down the back of her arm until it cupped her elbow and drew her closer to him. "You did. And I'm grateful for that. I'm grateful that we've become friends. But you know I want us to be so much more than that."

"We are."

"We are, but we're not yet everything I want us to be."

Her heart felt as though it might beat out of her chest. Was he asking ... was he saying that he wanted them to be ...? She looked up into his eyes.

He was. There was no mistaking the love in his eyes. He loved her. She knew it; she could see it. He'd done everything he could to prove it to her. And now those big, brown eyes were pleading with her. Asking her to say that she wanted it, too.

He raised his glass and held it out to her. "New beginnings?"

She held his gaze and nodded. "New beginnings."

Diego took a drink of his champagne and set his glass down. He'd almost asked a different question. He believed that if he asked her now, she'd say yes. But it wasn't the right time yet.

He needed to make it special. He needed her to know not only how much he loved her but also how well he understood her. He knew her hang-ups, and he needed her to know that he planned to spend the rest of his life helping her past them.

"There you are!" He turned to see Zack and Maria coming out onto the deck. "Kenzie said you were here, but we couldn't find you."

Diego smiled at his son, glad that he hadn't asked Izzy that other question. He wanted Zack and Maria to be there when he did. Them and Ted and Audrey. All the people who he considered to be family—and everyone he wanted Izzy to know as her family, too. "We were making the most of the quiet before we get the party started."

Zack laughed and looked at Izzy. "I hope you like to dance? It's tough to keep up with him when he wants to party."

Izzy laughed and patted Diego's cheek. "No worries there. He's the one who needs to keep up." She picked up her glass and slipped her arm through Maria's. "Come on, let's go find everyone, shall we?"

Diego winked at Zack as they followed them back inside. "She's not kidding, you know."

"I didn't think she was. I get the feeling that you and I are going to spend a lot of time trailing after those two in the years to come."

Diego nodded happily. "I believe we will."

They found Ted and Audrey sitting with her kids, Ally and Brayden, and a bunch of Zack's friends. Diego smiled when he saw Austin. "You made it then?"

"I did."

Diego looked around at the others who were sitting with them. He knew Zack's best friend, Luke, and his fiancée,

Angel. Roxy, who worked at the lodge, was there, too, with her fiancé, Logan, who was building Ted's house.

Colt, the deputy who'd worked with Manny to help Zack finally take Morales down, was sitting in between his lady, Cassie, and Austin. He greeted Diego with a smile. "Have you heard from Manny?"

"I have. You need to help me. We need to do everything we can to convince him to stay when he comes up here."

Colt grinned. "I'm down with that. Manny's awesome."

Maria nodded. "I love that man."

"Hey!" Zack gave her a stern look, but there was laughter in his eyes. "How many times do I have to tell you?"

Maria laughed. "You can tell me as often as you like, but it's not going to change the fact that Manny is a great guy." She waggled her eyebrows at the other girls and added, "Or the fact that he's one sexy silver fox."

Zack threw his hands in the air. "What am I supposed to do?"

Diego chuckled. "You might just need to admit that with age comes a certain something that you younger guys just can't compete with."

He'd only meant to joke with the guys, but as he said it, he wondered what Izzy would think. He held his breath as he caught her eye, hoping that she wasn't going to be mad at him.

He needn't have worried. She was smiling and nodding. "I hate to admit it, but he's right."

His heart buzzed in his chest. She wasn't just playing along with the conversation. She was reassuring him. He hadn't thought he was someone who needed reassurance—about anything, from anyone. But it meant the world to him that she understood the one reservation he'd had about her.

"I take it he's a bit of a ladies' man?" asked Austin.

"No." Diego and Zack spoke at the same time and then laughed.

"He's not," said Diego.

"Even though the ladies would like him to be." Zack gave Maria another mock scowl as he said it, but she just smiled sweetly at him and shrugged.

"He's been too busy with work most of his life to bother with women," said Diego. "But apparently, he's thinking about taking early retirement."

"What does he do?" asked Izzy.

"He works for the FBI. He's been the Special Agent in Charge of the Sacramento field office for the last few years."

"He's a great guy," said Colt.

"I remember him," said Austin. "I didn't make the connection when he called me about finding a short-term rental, but he's the guy who was here to help you, right, Zack? The one I met when you bought your place."

"That's right."

Izzy was watching the conversation, and it made Diego realize that he'd never told her what had happened with Zack. She knew that the two of them hadn't seen much of each other for years, but she didn't know why or how the situation had been resolved. He shuddered at the thought of it. He'd spent all those years hoping and praying that he wouldn't lose his son.

"And he's moving here, too?" she asked.

Diego grinned at Zack. "It seems I might have the same problem you do, and Izzy hasn't even met him yet."

She slapped his arm. "I thought you were God's gift to women, and no other guy could compete?"

He laughed. "I am. It's poor Manny I'm worried about, having to fend off your advances."

She laughed. "He's got no worries. I just like to keep you on your toes."

"Don't I know it."

~ ~ ~

It was after midnight by the time they made their way outside with Audrey and Ted.

"Well, that was fun," said Audrey.

"It was," Izzy agreed. "Who'd have thought that first time we came here that things would work out like this?"

Diego slung his arm around her shoulders. "I hoped they would."

She laughed. "Nope. Not buying that. Your hopes that night only went as far as the next morning."

He gave the others an innocent look. "Do you even know what she's talking about?"

"They do. But they're far too polite to admit it."

Ted smiled at her. "I can vouch for the fact that it wasn't very long before he was hoping that things would work out this way. And he's not the only one who's happy that they have."

He was such a good guy. She went and kissed his cheek and then hugged Audrey. "I'd say we're all happy about it."

Audrey nodded. "We are."

"Do you guys want us to get the cab to drop you off?" asked Ted.

Diego looked down at her, but Izzy shook her head. "I love that we can walk home from here."

He winked at her, and she knew what he meant—she'd called it home again. And it made her happy to realize that she saw it that way already.

He put his arm around her shoulders as they crossed the square. "It was a great night, don't you think?"

"It was. I love that everyone hangs out together here. You and Zack, Ted and Eddie. Audrey and Ally and Brayden. Back in Ventura, they'd come over to her place all the time, but they rarely came out with us."

"It seems to be the way here. I like it, too. You and Maria seem to have hit it off."

She smiled. "Yeah. She's a sweetheart. I can see why Zack adores her."

He laughed. "She said the same thing about you."

"She did? What that you adore me?"

"No. That Zack does."

"He does?" She'd had a few laughs with him this afternoon and tonight. She knew he didn't have a problem with her, but to hear that he adored her made her happy.

"Of course, he does. You're adorable. And he can see how happy you make me." He dropped a kiss on her lips. "He can see how much I love you."

She looked up into his eyes. "I hope he can see how much I love you."

# Chapter Eighteen

When the plane landed at the Santa Paula airport, Diego took hold of Izzy's hand. "Do you want me to come with you? We could get your things together today then head back to my house later. I only need to go into the office for a few hours. I could do that in the morning and then we can go back to the lake tomorrow afternoon."

"No. It's okay. Let's stick with the plan. I need to do some work today." She smiled. "And I won't get around to it if you're with me. And besides, if you go into the office today, then we can go home in the morning."

He had to smile at the way she kept calling it home. "Okay. I'll get back here as early as I can."

"Just let me know what time you're coming, and I'll come and pick you up."

"I could rent a car."

She shook her head. "You've been doing far too much of that. In fact, I was thinking I should probably drive up to the lake next time we come back here. That way, I'll have my car up there."

He frowned. "We can talk about it." He held her gaze. It was time to at least make the suggestion. "I was thinking that maybe we should have second cars there."

She laughed. "I don't need a second car."

"Perhaps not. But I'd like you to have one."

She met his gaze. He didn't see the flash of anger that he'd grown used to whenever she felt he was overstepping. He relaxed when she smiled. "That's sweet of you, but it doesn't make any sense. If I'm going to be up at the lake ..." She squeezed his hand. "And I plan to be, then I should take my car up there."

"Can we talk about it?"

The plane came to a stop. "We can, but not now." She nodded at the cockpit door, and Karl came out and smiled at them.

"Did you guys decide if we're here for a while?"

Izzy smiled back at him. "No. I'm bailing. You can take this guy away again."

Diego laughed and shook his head at Karl. "She's trying to get rid of me, but you'll bring me back later, won't you?"

"I will." Karl looked at Izzy. "You might be able to bail on him for the day, but I don't think you'll get away with any longer than that."

When he turned to let down the steps, Diego planted a kiss on her lips. "He's right, you know."

"I'm glad."

He got to his feet and followed her down the steps.

"Where are you going?"

He laughed. "I'm seeing you to your car."

"There's no need. I'm a big girl. You should get going. The sooner you go, the sooner you can come back."

He shook his head. "No. You can boss me around to some extent. I'll try to be good about most things, but I'm not leaving here until I've seen you back to your car."

She pursed her lips, and he wondered if she was about to argue. He was relieved when she smiled. "Okay, come on then. And don't think you've won. I'm gracefully accepting that you're just being a gentleman."

He took her hand as they walked back across the tarmac. "I am a gentleman." He winked and added, "Most of the time."

When they reached her car, he backed her up against it and cupped the sides of her neck between his hands. He looked down at her lips. They were plump and pink. He brushed his over them and felt her relax against him. He kissed her deeply; he couldn't help it. It didn't matter that they were standing in the middle of a parking lot. It wouldn't matter where they were. Whenever he kissed her, she made him want more. Her kisses were intoxicating.

When he lifted his head, she smiled up at him. "Damn, you can kiss."

He laughed. "I was thinking the same thing about you."

"Want to come back with me and make good on what that kiss just promised?"

He laughed. "Absolutely. It was you who said I couldn't. I'm up for it."

She touched the front of his pants and smiled. "I know! I could feel how up for it you are!"

He shrugged. "What can I say? The way you kiss me makes me not want to be a gentleman anymore."

She reached up and pecked his lips. "You can remind me just how ungentlemanly you can be when you get back here tonight."

He gave her a sad look. "You were only joking about me coming back with you?"

"Yeah. I'd love you to come, but it'd mess everything up."

He smirked. "But I want to come now." He pressed his hips against her to make his point clear.

She laughed. "You wicked man! Don't tempt me. Go on, get going before I give in to you. You can come tonight."

He cupped her cheek in his hand. "So can you."

She turned her face and kissed his hand. "I have no doubt I will. Let me know what time you'll be back, and I'll be here waiting."

"Okay. I love you, Izzy."

"I love you. See you later."

Izzy pulled the car into the garage when she got home. She'd have to remember to park it in here when they left tomorrow. She didn't want to leave it out on the driveway because she didn't know when she'd be back. She smiled. That felt good. It didn't scare her, and she didn't have any reservations. It was all good. Diego loved her. She loved him. They were at the beginning of their journey together, and she trusted him that wherever this journey took them, he was in it with her.

She let herself in and looked around the kitchen. It was funny. She'd lived here for six years. It was the only house she'd owned after her divorce. She'd had some good times here, but now, everywhere she looked, she could see Diego. He'd eclipsed all the other memories this house had held. She could see him cooking for her. See him standing at the bottom of the stairs beckoning for her to go with him. She knew how lucky she was.

She went to the fridge and poured herself a glass of water. She loved that he knew how lucky he was, too. She sat down at the counter and pulled her phone out. She needed to send a couple of emails out to clients. She frowned when she saw one from Rafa. Bless him. She'd thought that he would have given up and moved on by now.

She sent him a quick reply, telling him that she'd met someone else, that she wished him well, but nothing was ever going to happen between them again. She truly did wish him well.

After she'd done that, she got busy with work. Audrey had told her to take some time off if she wanted, and she was thinking she might just do that. She wanted to tie up loose ends today. She and Diego were going back to the lake tomorrow, and she was hoping that they might take the rest of the week to just get used to being there—to being together.

She stopped to make herself a sandwich for lunch. She'd need to sort the fridge out before she left. She didn't want to leave things in there to go moldy. She knew she'd be back, but she didn't know when. Diego kept calling the house at the lake their house, kept saying that they were going to live there. They hadn't really talked about the details of what that meant, but she was up for it. As far as she was concerned now, she was all in with him.

She smiled when she remembered the time they'd been waiting for the minibus to collect them from the lodge to come home. There'd been a rainbow, and he'd asked if she wanted to find the crock of gold with him. He was such a romantic like that.

At the time, though, she hadn't realized it. She'd told him that the only thing at the end of the rainbow was a crock of shit. She felt bad about that now. Still, hopefully, she'd have all the time in the world to make it up to him—the rest of her life if things worked out the way it looked like they would.

The afternoon flew by, and the next time she looked at her watch, it was six-thirty. She frowned. She'd have expected him to call before now to let her know what time he'd be back. Still, he had a lot to do himself. He'd gone to the office, and he'd gone home to get more clothes to bring to the lake. She frowned. And he needed to check in with Carmen, too.

It didn't bother her that he had a housekeeper. It wasn't surprising that he'd need help to keep that big house clean. She liked him for it if she was honest. She liked the story of how he'd taken her on as a babysitter when he was young, single dad and how she'd stayed with him and Zack ever since. She was looking forward to meeting her.

She looked up at the sound of a car door outside. Had he rented himself a car? She ran to the front door and opened it with a big smile on her face.

That smile faded when she saw that it wasn't him. It was Rafa.

"Hi, Izzy."

"What are you doing here?"

"I wanted to talk to you."

She blew out a sigh. "We've said all we need to say, Rafa."

"I know you think so, but ..." He shrugged. "Can we? Can I come in?"

She nodded reluctantly. If this was what it would take to give him some closure, then she owed him that. "Okay."

He followed her through to the kitchen. "I know you said you've met someone else. But what did I do wrong?"

"Nothing! You didn't do anything wrong, sweetheart. You're a good guy. It's not you—"

He held up a hand. "Please don't give me the *it's not you, it's me* speech."

She chuckled. "Okay, then. I won't. But in this case, it happens to be the truth. I was honest with you from the beginning, Rafa. I wasn't looking for anything serious. We were just for fun. Just physical."

"I know. You were straight with me about that, but I didn't think you meant it."

"Why not?"

He shrugged and gave her a sad smile. "Maybe because I'm an idiot? I must be."

"No, you're not. You're a good guy. And you'll meet someone else—someone who's right for you."

"I think you're right for me."

"I'm not. I'm way too old for you."

He pursed his lips. "Age doesn't make any difference, not if you don't want it to."

She stared at him for a moment. He had a point there.

"You told me you weren't interested in anything serious, but now you're telling me that you've met someone else. Is that serious?"

She nodded.

"That's what makes me want to know what I did wrong. I don't mean to make this difficult for you. I just want to understand. What does he have that I don't?"

She couldn't help but chuckle. "One of the most important things he has is about twenty years more life experience."

"Oh. He's old then?"

She laughed. "Yeah. I suppose to you he is. But to me, he's just right, and I love him."

He nodded sadly. "That's not something I can do anything about, is it?"

"It isn't. Listen, I'm sorry, Rafa."

"I'm the one who's sorry."

Izzy jumped, and they both turned to see Diego standing in the kitchen doorway. She couldn't make out what the expression on his face meant. Was he mad? Her heart started to race. Please, God, don't let him be mad. Don't let him think this was something it wasn't.

He took a step toward Rafa, and her heart jumped into her throat. What was he going to do? She slid down from her stool in a panic. She relaxed when he held his hand out to Rafa and gave him a friendly smile.

Rafa shook with him.

"I'll never say I'm sorry that Izzy chose me over you." He smiled at her. "I'll be forever grateful that she did. I'm sorry for you that you lost out on the wonderful person she is. You'll meet someone else. I wish you happiness. But you'll never meet someone like her."

Rafa nodded. "I know." He gave Izzy a sad smile. "I guess I got my answers. I should go."

Izzy went to him and gave him a quick hug. She didn't miss the way Diego's eyebrows came down when she did it, but he could deal with it.

Once Rafa had gone, she raised her eyebrows at Diego. "I thought you were going to call me."

"And I thought you wanted me out of the way so that you could work."

She sucked in a deep breath. What was he saying?

He came to her and closed his arms around her. "Sorry. I take that back. That was just a little bit of jealousy creeping in, and I apologize."

She rested her cheek against his chest. "Apology accepted. And I apologize, too. That can't have been easy—to walk in and see him here. How much did you hear?"

He leaned back so he could see her face, and then he smirked. "I heard that I might seem old to him, but that you think I'm perfect, and you love me."

She laughed and slapped his arm. "You and your huge ego! I said that you're just right, not that you're perfect."

He grinned. "But you did tell him that you love me."

She nodded. "I did because I do."

"And when you said I'm just right, did you mean I'm the perfect fit?" He was pressing himself against her, and she knew damned well what he meant.

"I don't know about that."

"No?" He raised an eyebrow at her. "Do I need to remind you just how perfectly we fit together?" He closed his hand around the back of her neck, sending shivers of anticipation running through her.

"I think perhaps you do."

He took her hand and led her to the stairs. She stopped and went to lock the front door before she went with him. "I don't think we want anyone else coming in unannounced, do we?"

He chuckled. "We don't."

As he lay there with her wrapped up in his arms afterward, Diego held her closer to his chest. She looked up into his eyes.

"Are you okay?"

He nodded.

"What is it, though? Are you still thinking about Rafa being here?"

"No. Well, yes, but not in the way you think."

She leaned back so she could get a better look at him. "I'm sorry. But it didn't mean anything."

"I know, mi amor. I trust you completely. It's not that."

"What then?"

He held her gaze for a long moment, wondering if he should tell her what he was thinking. He knew he'd have to. "I don't want this to come out the wrong way. Forgive me if I choose the wrong words?"

"I'll try."

"What you told me about ..." His heart was racing as he thought about it. He wanted to kill the bastard. "About your foster father."

Her lips pressed together. "What about it?"

"I can't imagine. I'm sorry."

"I've told you. I don't want you to feel sorry for me." She started to pull away, but he held onto her, and to his relief, she relaxed. "Sorry, go on. Whatever you want to know, ask."

"It's just. I would have thought that experience might have put you off men—sex. But you ..." How the hell was he supposed to say that she seemed to like it more than most women he'd known?

She surprised him with a smile. "It's okay. You think I should be traumatized or terrified of men, or at the very least, I should have been put off sex for life, right?"

He nodded and dropped a kiss on the tip of her nose.

"It's okay. I asked myself that same question for a long time. I ... when I went to college, let's say I was popular with the boys."

He closed his eyes for a moment, not wanting to think about it.

"I only figured it out in therapy years later. He ..." She blew out a sigh. "He used to tell me that I belonged to him. That I was his. That no other man would ever touch me. I wasn't allowed to have boyfriends." She didn't look sad or angry, just resigned as she continued. "As soon as I got out of that house, I guess I rebelled against him. I made the most of my freedom. One of the therapists I saw told me that it's common for women who've been abused as girls to become promiscuous later in life." She looked up into his eyes. "I don't like to think of myself as promiscuous, but I wasn't exactly a nun."

He nodded. "So, the thing with younger guys was about having boyfriends like you weren't allowed to?"

"I guess."

"And the thing about avoiding big macho guys like me was about avoiding what reminded you of him?"

She nodded.

"And you think that you're going to be okay with me?"

She looked up into his eyes. His heart felt as though it might break in two when she shook her head. He'd understand if she felt she couldn't do it. It'd kill him, but he'd respect it. He loved her too much to hurt her any more than she'd already been hurt.

"I'm not just okay with you, Diego. I love you. You're the best thing that's ever happened to me. You've gotten me over the last of it without even knowing how much you've helped me. You've made me see that it can't touch me anymore." She planted a kiss on his lips. "I'm not afraid of you. When I told you that in the beginning, it was a lie, even though I didn't know it. I was afraid of you, or at least of everything you reminded me of. But being with you has shown me that what I was afraid of is a ghost of the past. And what I have with you is the present." She smiled. "And hopefully, the future."

He held her close and kissed her. That was the best way he knew to tell her everything he was feeling. When he finally lifted his head, he looked down into her eyes. "You are my future, Izzy. If you want me."

"I do."

# Chapter Nineteen

It was raining as Diego sat in his new office on Thursday morning. This room was one of the things that he'd fallen in love with when he first looked at the house. It was probably better named a study than an office. It was done all in rich woods; the walls were lined with bookcases, and the huge desk looked out across the lawns to the lake.

When Izzy had first visited his house in Laguna Beach, he'd told her that he liked sleek modern architecture, and he did. But that was partly because traditional architecture had always felt like it was part of a world that was out of his reach. He'd grown up poor in Colombia. His mother used to clean the church and the Padre's house, too. When he was small, he'd gone with her sometimes. The Padre's office had been a lot like this room. He shook his head to clear it, wondering why he was dwelling on that when he was supposed to be calling Ted.

This would be their first regular morning call in a while, and the first he'd make from his new office.

He dialed the number and waited, checking the clock as he did. It was seven o'clock on the dot. Perhaps a sign that things were getting back to normal—or at least, that they might be establishing a new normal.

Ted answered on the first ring. "Buenos días, mi amigo."

Diego laughed. "Hola, buenos días."

"Are you settled in at the house?"

"We are."

"That's good. I'm happy for you. And dare I ask where it goes from here?"

"It's going where you hoped it would. In fact, what are you doing this afternoon?"

"Whatever you tell me I'm doing."

"Then I'm picking you up at three-thirty, and you're coming over to Four Mile with me."

"Are we meeting the girls?"

"No. We're going shopping."

"For?"

"I'll tell you when I get there."

"You can tell me now if it's what I think it is."

"What do you think it is?"

"Are we going shopping at the store where Maria works?"

Diego had to laugh. "Yes, we are."

"That's awesome, Diego. I'm so happy for you."

"Perhaps you should save the congratulations until Sunday?"

"What, you have doubts? That's not like you."

"No. I don't really doubt. But Lady Luck has been so good to me, I don't want to take anything for granted."

"I don't think you need to worry."

"Neither do I, but I'll still be happier on Sunday once I know for sure."

"Okay. I won't say anything else." Ted laughed. "Other than tell you I can't wait to go shopping with you. I never thought I'd see the day I'd say that. But I can't wait to see what you pick. I know you; I know your taste."

Diego grinned. "I need to find something special."

"I'm sure you will."

"Okay. Enough of that. Back to work, mi amigo. How have things been going while I've been slacking?"

Izzy smiled when she passed Diego's office and heard him laughing. He'd said he was going to get back into his routine this morning. And part of his routine was talking to Ted at seven each day. She loved that they had such a good friendship. It made her want to talk to Audrey. But they wouldn't do that until a little later.

She went into the kitchen and found a note sticking out from under the coffee pot.

*Sorry I had to get started before you came down.*

*I made you pancakes. They're in the warmer.*

*I love you. Oxoxoxo*

Her heart felt as though it melted a little bit as she read it. How did such a big, macho guy get to be so damned sweet?

She didn't need to know how; she was just grateful that he was. And she was fully aware of how lucky she was, that she was the woman he'd fallen in love with.

She poured herself some coffee and went to get the pancakes from the warmer drawer. She sat at the counter to eat them and watched the rain fall. It wasn't heavy; it spotted the lake as the drops landed in the water.

The rain had always made her feel sad, but not this morning. This morning she didn't think there was anything that could dampen the happiness she felt.

"Good morning, mi amor."

She turned and smiled when he came into the kitchen. "Hey. I thought you were talking to Ted."

"I did. We're good for now. I'm going to see him this afternoon."

"Oh, okay."

"What are you doing today?"

She smiled. "Right now, I'm just watching the rain fall."

"Isn't it beautiful?"

She laughed. "You think everything's beautiful."

He grinned. "I do. Because it is. The whole world is beautiful when you're in love."

She rolled her eyes. "Seriously?"

He gave her a sheepish look. "Too much?"

She nodded. "I mean, it's lovely that you're so enthusiastic, but you might be going just a touch overboard."

He straightened up and looked all serious. "Very well. I shall behave in a manner more befitting my age."

She laughed. "Don't do that. I love you just the way you are."

He came and closed his arms around her. "And I love you, Miss Isobel. I'm just so happy."

"I am, too."

"You didn't look completely happy when I came in here."

"I was. I was thinking about the rain. It usually makes me feel sad for some reason."

He raised an eyebrow at her. "It does?"

"Yeah, but not today." She downed the last of her coffee. "Today, I have too much to do to sit around being sad. I'm going to go to the grocery store. Do you want anything?"

"We can go together?"

"No. You have to work. And besides, I don't plan to let you do everything around here." She smiled at him. "You keep saying this is our house, and if it is, then I want to be able to shop and cook as well."

He smiled. "Whatever you want. We're going to figure out how we want this to work, how we want to work together."

"We are. And what I want today is to go grocery shopping and to make you dinner tonight."

"Thank you. I'm going to see Ted this afternoon, but I should be back by five-thirty. Six at the latest."

She laughed. "I want to make you dinner, not turn into a nag. You'll be here when you get here. That'll be fine whenever it is."

"It's not about nagging, Miss Isobel, it's about becoming a team. Teams need to communicate if they're going to work well together."

"You're right. Don't mind me. I think I'm just a little bit nervous about getting this right."

He tucked his fingers under her chin and tilted it so she looked up into his eyes. "Don't be nervous, mi amor, we'll get it right ... together."

It was ten o'clock by the time she made it to the grocery store. Diego had hung around and had coffee with her, then Audrey had called because she'd lost track of one of the client files.

Izzy smiled as she got out of the car. This felt like real life. Doing everyday stuff like this here at Summer Lake was what it was going to take to make her feel like this wasn't just some happy little interlude, some extended vacation that would end soon and send her back to Ventura.

She took a cart and made her way to the produce aisle. A little girl came to stand beside her while she was looking at the bananas.

"They're good for you. Did you know that? They have 'tassium, and your body needs 'tassium."

Izzy smiled at her. She was a cute little thing with a blonde ponytail. "I knew they were good for you, but I didn't know why. Do you like them?"

The girl nodded. "I never used to. My mom used to say that fruits are too expensive, and they don't taste good enough. But

Cassie says when you do the math, fruits are cheaper than candy, and they're better for you. I still like candy, though."

Izzy laughed. "I'll bet you do." She looked around, wondering what this little chatterbox was doing here by herself. "Is your mom here?"

"No. She dumped me when she left town."

Izzy's heart started to race. What had she walked into?

She relaxed a little when the girl smiled. "I live with Cassie and Colt now. They're my new mom and dad."

She knew who Colt and Cassie were. They'd been at the Boathouse with everyone last weekend. Colt was the sheriff's deputy. "Are they your foster parents?" At least the kid had lucked out being placed with a deputy and a doctor. She'd fared much better than Izzy had.

"No. Kelly said I was going to end up in the system, but Cassie and Colt didn't want that, so they adopted me."

"Wow."

The girl grinned at her. "I know. I'm lucky, right?"

Izzy had to laugh. The kid was quite a character. "You are. And I bet Cassie and Colt think they're lucky, too."

"They tell me that all the time."

"Sophie!"

They both turned to see Cassie hurrying toward them. "How many times do I have to tell you not to wander off?"

"Sorry." She smiled at Izzy. "I made a new friend."

Cassie shot Izzy an apologetic look. Then she recognized her. "Oh, hi. It's Izzy, isn't it?"

"That's right, and you're Cassie. Sorry, I kept Sophie. We got to talking."

Sophie shot her a grateful smile.

"That's okay. But we really need to get going. Come on, Sophie."

The kid smiled at Izzy. "Do you want to be my friend?"

Izzy nodded. "Sure."

"Sophie!"

She could tell that Cassie didn't want the kid to be rude, but Izzy felt a kinship with her, and it seemed that it was mutual. "It's okay." She smiled at Cassie, hoping she might understand, even though she wasn't sure she understood it herself. "Sophie and I just realized we have some things in common."

Cassie came back a few steps. "You do?"

"Yeah. Our background." She gave her a meaningful look and was relieved when understanding dawned on her face.

"Oh. I see."

Sophie looked up at her. "You were adopted, too?"

"No. I never got that lucky."

"Can I come to your house one day?"

Cassie gave Izzy an apologetic look. "You don't just invite yourself over like that, Sophie."

Izzy smiled. "It's okay." She looked at Sophie. "You have to ask Cassie. But if she ever needs someone to watch you for a while, you're welcome to come over."

Sophie grinned at Cassie. "Can I?"

Cassie smiled. "We'll see. It's very kind of you."

"I mean it. I just moved here, and I don't know many people yet. I know you know Diego, so it's not like I'm just some strange woman you met at the store."

Cassie laughed. "Far from it. I do know Diego, and I've gotten to know Audrey, too. Zack and Maria think you're wonderful. It seems like the whole town has been waiting for you to get here. I feel honored that you'd let Sophie come over. Don't think you have to, though."

"Like I said. We have something in common. We might be good for each other."

"Thanks." Cassie nodded. "I might need to take you up on the offer to watch her next week. If you really don't mind."

"I'd love it. I'll give you my number."

After Cassie had taken her number, Sophie came and took hold of her hand. "Can I call you Aunt Izzy?"

Izzy had to swallow around the lump in her throat. She nodded.

"Thanks, Aunt Izzy. I don't have any family left here. You can be mine." With that, she smiled and skipped away.

Cassie watched her go. "Sorry about that. She had it rough. She's finding her feet now, but until she said that, I had no idea how she felt about family."

Izzy's throat burned when she spoke. "It's okay. I totally understand how she feels. I'll look forward to getting to know her ... and to being her Aunt Izzy."

Cassie smiled. "You should probably get used to it. It seems like everyone is family around here, in one way or another."

~ ~ ~

Diego felt like a kid who was excited for Christmas to come. He and Ted had done their shopping. Maria had assured him that he'd made the right choice. He kept taking it out to look at it. It was beautiful.

He shoved it back into his pocket quickly when he heard Izzy come in from the deck. She'd been on the phone with Audrey.

She'd seemed a little subdued when he got home. She'd made dinner for them—pasta, and it smelled wonderful. She'd gone out to talk to Audrey while he got changed.

He went to her and closed his arms around her. "How was your day?"

"It was good, thanks. How about you? How did you get on with Ted?"

He grinned. "It went very well." For a moment, he considered asking her right now, so that he could show her just how well he and Ted had done. But no. He had to wait until

Sunday. He'd talked to everyone, and they were all going to come over. Now all he had to do was figure out how he could get them here without her figuring out what was going on.

He realized that she wasn't relaxing against him like she normally did when he held her. "Are you sure you're okay?"

"I'm fine. Well …"

He leaned back so he could see her face. "What?"

"It's nothing. It's good, if anything."

He took her hand and went to sit on one of the chairs at the dining table. He patted his lap. "Tell me?"

She smiled and sat on his knee, looping her arms around his neck. "You have every reason to be full of yourself, don't you? You're such a good guy."

He grinned. "I'm glad you finally understand me. But tell me what's bothering you?"

"You know Cassie and Colt?"

"I do."

"Well, did you know that they adopted a little girl, Sophie?"

"I did. Zack told me all about it. She's a sweet little thing. I met her once." He smiled as he remembered. "She has a sailor's mouth, but I suppose that's to be expected, given her background."

"What do you know about her background?"

"That her mother left town with a boyfriend—a boyfriend who …" He looked at her. "Why are you asking?"

"Because I met her and Cassie in the store today. She took a shine to me. I don't know, it felt like I recognized something in her, or maybe she recognized something in me." She smiled. "She asked if I want to be her Aunt Izzy and if she could come over and visit sometime."

He smiled. "I hope you said, yes?"

"I did. I wasn't sure what you'd think, though."

"I love the idea. Colt and Cassie love her like their own, but I don't think she has any other family."

"She doesn't. She told me that. That's why she wanted to call me Aunt Izzy."

"It sounds like she wants you to be her Aunt Izzy, not just to call you that."

She nodded.

"Are you unhappy about it somehow?"

"No! God no! I love the idea. I guess I'm just struggling with the whole family thing myself."

"What's to struggle with, Miss Isobel?"

She looked down into his eyes, and he felt his heart fill up with love for her.

"Nothing. There's nothing left to struggle with, is there? If I can just lean into it. If I can accept how lucky I am to have found you. How lucky I am that you love me the way you do. Then there's no struggle left."

He smiled. "And yet, you're struggling to believe it?"

She shrugged.

"What would it take for you to relax and accept it?"

"I don't know. Probably just time."

He nodded. He hoped that what he planned to do on Sunday would help move things along.

# Chapter Twenty

Audrey grinned at Izzy. "Have you told Diego about his competition yet?"

He narrowed his eyes at her. "I have competition?"

She laughed. "As if that would worry you."

"It might." He took hold of her hand and brought it up to his lips, brushing them over her wrist.

She shivered as he did it. It got to her every time, and he knew it.

"Tell me."

She rolled her eyes. "Audrey is teasing me because I've never made a secret of the fact that I think Clay McAdam is a good-looking man."

He smirked. "That's okay. I agree. I think he's a good-looking man, too. I'm not going to throw my panties at him, though. And I hope you're not thinking about doing anything like that."

She laughed. "In my younger days, maybe. Not anymore, though."

"I don't think Marianne would be too impressed if you did," said Ted. He nodded toward the deck where Marianne and

Clay were coming in with Seymour Davenport and his lady, Chris.

Diego waved at them and called them over. Then he raised an eyebrow at her. "I hope I can trust you to be a good girl?"

She laughed. "As long as I can trust you to be a good boy."

"Always."

"Hey, everyone." Clay smiled around at them. "How are you doing?"

"Great, thanks. Do you want to join us?" Diego asked.

Izzy hadn't been expecting that, but she probably should have. They all knew each other. Even Audrey had become friends with Marianne and Chris since she'd moved up here.

Clay looked at Marianne, and she smiled. "I'd love to."

"So would we," said Chris.

"I'll hang with you while I can," said Clay. "But I'm going to get up with the guys to do a set tonight."

"We'd heard. In fact, you're the reason Izzy's here."

Clay smiled at her. He really was a good-looking guy. He was no Diego, but still!

"It's nice to finally meet you, Izzy. I've heard so much about you." He held his hand out, and she shook with him, and then the others.

Seymour smiled her and then at Diego. "I, for one, want to thank you. Now that you're here, I know that this man will stick around."

She looked up at Diego, and he dropped a kiss on her lips. He seemed to read her mind as he so often did. "What can I say? They're my friends. And I can't help talking about you."

"All the time," said Chris with a smile. "I hope you're going to come out for lunch with me, now that you're here?"

Izzy nodded. She loved the idea. She knew that Audrey had lunch with the two women sometimes. It seemed that she was closer to Marianne than Chris, but she'd told Izzy several times that she couldn't wait to get her and Chris together. "I'd love that."

Clay looked around. "Is Eddie here, Ted? I want to ask him what we're doing."

Ted laughed. "You know what they're like. They'll play whatever you tell them to. It's good of you to do this."

Clay laughed. "As far as I'm concerned, it's good of them to let me get up with them."

Izzy watched the conversation go around. It seemed like the four men were good friends. She hadn't realized they were as close as they seemed to be.

Diego moved his leg against hers, and she looked up at him. He raised an eyebrow, and she nodded. She wasn't used to being the quiet one in a group, but she was just finding her feet here, with these guys. She loved Diego for noticing and checking in with her.

"Are your kids coming tonight?" Marianne asked Audrey.

"Brayden is. I'm not sure about Ally. She said something about one of her friends being upset, so she was going to see her."

"Oh." Chris frowned. "Which one?"

"She didn't say, and I got the impression that was deliberate." Audrey smiled. "Now, I understand why. I'm finally figuring out how small towns work. If she'd told me, I'd be able to tell you, and you would no doubt know the friend, too, and you'd worry about her."

Chris smiled. "That's right. The only trouble now, though, is that I'm going to worry and not know who I'm worrying about."

Izzy wondered what it must be like to not only have your kids around, but to have their friends around, too, and be invested in their lives. It wasn't something she'd ever known, but she imagined it would be kind of cool.

Clay looked at her, and she could only hope that he wasn't about to ask if she had kids. He didn't. "How are you doing with small-town life?"

She smiled. "I'm getting the hang of it. I like it so far."

He had such a kind smile. "I didn't think I'd ever want to live in a small town again, but I love this place." He put his arm around Marianne's shoulders. "I'm happier here than I've ever been."

Seymour nodded. "I'm the same. I'm not exactly a small-town kind of guy, but I love it here." He smiled at her. "You'll get used to it."

"You will," agreed Chris. "Especially if you start coming out with me." She made a face at Diego. "You can't keep her to yourself all the time."

Izzy laughed when he wrapped his arms around her. "I know. She wouldn't let me if I tried. I'm banking on you guys to help me keep her happy here."

They all laughed, and Izzy couldn't help snuggling a little closer against him. He was doing such a good job of making her feel at home.

He looked around at them all. "In fact, do you all want to come over to our place tomorrow afternoon? We could have a little housewarming." He looked at Izzy. "And you can get to know the ladies better."

She nodded and looked around at them. They were all nodding eagerly. She almost felt as though they knew something she didn't. She laughed. "Okay, let's do it."

~ ~ ~

Diego watched her as she chatted with Chris. He could see the two of them becoming friends. He liked Chris—she was nobody's fool.

He turned when he felt a hand come down on his shoulder. His son had learned that one from him.

"How's it going, Papá?"

He nodded. "Better than I even hoped. How about you?"

"Great. I'm enjoying watching you and Izzy. You're good together."

"I know." He met Zack's eye. "And you don't have any reservations about me doing this?"

"Hell, no! I'm excited." He chuckled. "Of course, I'm excited for you. And if you want to know the truth, I'm excited for me, too."

Diego raised an eyebrow at him.

"I barely remember my mother. It's been you and me most of my life. For a long time there, I barely had you. Now, I get you back, here in my life—and I get Izzy, too."

Diego had to blink away the tears that pricked behind his eyes. "I'm sorry."

"No! Don't be. I wouldn't have wanted a woman to come into our lives before now. It was just you and me. But now, maybe this is selfish, but now I have Maria, I want you to have someone in your life also. And since the someone you chose is Izzy, I'm excited for her to be a part of my life. She's not exactly the motherly kind, is she? But I couldn't handle it if she were."

Diego nodded. He didn't want to speak because he didn't trust himself.

"Did I say that right this time?"

"You did, mi hijo. You said it well."

"Good. Then don't go getting all emotional on me. Or I'll have to walk away ... before I join in!"

Diego had to laugh. "And we can't have that. We have to keep up appearances. We're supposed to be big, tough, macho guys, are we not?"

Zack laughed with him and jerked his head to the dance
floor where Izzy and Maria were dancing with some of the
other girls. "Perhaps we're supposed to be. But if anyone
knows better, it's those two."

Izzy looked over and smiled. Diego blew her a kiss. She
knew him better than that now, even if she hadn't believed it in
the beginning.

~ ~ ~

Izzy went out onto the deck and then came back in again.
There was nothing for her to do. Diego had called the catering
company this morning—even though she'd been convinced
that they wouldn't be able to help—not at this short notice on
a Sunday.

He came into the kitchen and smiled at her. "Relax. It's all
taken care of. The point of this is for you to have fun. I
wouldn't have done it if I thought it would stress you out like
this."

She made a face. "I'm not stressed. Well, maybe a little bit."

He came to her and closed his arms around her. "Relax."

She let out a shaky breath and rested her cheek against his
chest. That helped. It always did. Except he felt as though he
might be more stressed than she was. She looked up at him.
"What are you worried about?"

"What do you mean?"

She put her hand on his chest. "Your heart is pounding."

He smiled and dropped a kiss on her lips. "That's the effect
you have on me, Miss Isobel."

She wagged her finger at him. "I'm not buying your lines,
mister. What is it?"

He laughed. "Very well! I suppose I'm a little nervous, also.
But only because I want you to enjoy this. I want you to be

happy here." He looked more serious. "I want you to be happy with me in this life that we're building together."

"Aww. I am. I love you. You know I do."

He nodded. "I do."

She looked outside; it had been threatening to rain all morning. "Do you think we should have them move the food inside?"

"It'll be fine. They can move it if it rains. We don't need to look for problems before they arrive."

"True. What time are Zack and Maria coming?"

"They're on their way. He called a few minutes ago."

As if to answer her question, the doorbell rang, and they went together to answer it.

Zack and Maria stood there, grinning at them.

"Come on in," said Izzy. "You really don't need to ring the bell."

Zack smiled at her. "It seemed rude to just come in, but you're right. We're family, after all."

She smiled back at him. He'd gone out of his way to be nice to her last night, and it seemed he was doing the same today. She wrapped him in a hug. She liked him a lot.

Maria pushed him aside and hugged her next. "I'm the one who's big on family around here. I should be in on the hugs."

Izzy laughed and hugged her back. She loved that they were both so openly affectionate.

The doorbell rang again. This time it was Ted and Audrey. After that, people started arriving in droves, and Izzy had to give up and just relax and enjoy herself.

She was sitting chatting with Chris when little Sophie came running to her. "Aunt Izzy!" She climbed straight up into her lap and planted a kiss on her cheek.

Chris laughed. "I didn't know you had family here."

Izzy smiled. "Neither did I, but this young lady claimed me." She dropped a kiss on Sophie's head. "And I claimed her right back."

Colt and Cassie appeared. "Sorry," said Colt. "She's been so excited to come see her Aunt Izzy."

Izzy smiled. "No reason to be sorry. I've been looking forward to seeing her, too."

Diego appeared beside them, and to Izzy's surprise, Sophie cowered against her. Her arms instinctively tightened around her.

Diego nodded. He looked sad, but he understood. He took Colt's arm, and they walked away.

Izzy put her head down near Sophie's ear. "Did he remind you of someone?"

She nodded.

"Who?"

"Jimmy. My mom's boyfriend. He broke my arm."

Izzy's eyes filled with tears at the same time her heart raced. "Well, you can trust me that Diego is nothing like Jimmy. He's big and strong, but he's the kind of big and strong who looks out for little girls, not the kind that hurts them."

Sophie looked at her. "Are you sure?"

She nodded. "I can promise you."

"Okay." Sophie giggled. "He is handsome. Jimmy was butt ugly."

Izzy had to laugh. It seemed she truly had found a kindred spirit.

She looked around when she realized that the chatter had died down. It seemed everyone had stopped talking, and they were all looking at Diego, who was coming back to her with a big smile on his face. He held his hand out to her. She hadn't expected him to want to make some kind of speech or anything, but if he was going to, she was glad he wanted her with him when he did.

She set Sophie down and went to him. Chris gave her a
weird look as she went.

"Miss Isobel."

She looked up at him. He looked weird, too. He was smiling,
but his eyes were too shiny. Was he about to cry?

She went to him and wrapped her arms around him. "Are
you all right?"

He chuckled. "I am." He looked around, and she realized
that everyone was watching them. She stepped away from him,
but he kept hold of her hand.

"There's something I need to ask you."

She glanced around the room, wondering what was going on.
She caught Zack's eye, and he nodded and gave her an
encouraging smile. Maria was grinning by his side. Then she
spotted Audrey. Ted had his arm around her shoulders, and
she was wringing her hands together. Izzy couldn't understand
the look she gave her. She looked happy and nervous at the
same time.

"Miss Isobel?"

She looked back at Diego, and he laughed.

"This is kind of important. If I could have your attention?"

She laughed. "Sorry. I'm just wondering what you're setting
me up for. I mean, this is obviously a setup, isn't it? Look at
them all." She laughed again. "They're giving you away."

He did look around at everyone, but he chuckled and held
his hands up. "You see what I have to deal with? Now you
understand why I had to do it this way."

They all laughed with him, and Izzy felt even more confused.
"Do what? What are you up to?"

He took her hand and brought it up to his lips, brushing
them over her wrist before he spoke again. This time he was
more serious.

Her heart felt as though it might beat right out of her chest
when he got down on one knee. His big, brown eyes were full

of love as he looked up at her. "What I'm trying to do here, Miss Isobel is ask you to marry me. I asked you once not so long ago if you wanted to journey over the rainbow with me, to see if we might find the crock of gold." He looked around at everyone. "She told me it's a crock of shit!"

She had to laugh along with everyone. It was what she'd believed at the time. Since then, he'd proved her wrong.

"This time, I'm going to ask you in a simpler way. Just to be sure you understand. Izzy, I want you to walk through life beside me. I want to wake up with you every morning for the rest of our lives. I want to do everything in my power to make you happy. It won't all be rainbows and unicorn farts. Even a romantic like me can admit that. But I can promise you, it will be real. And if you'll have me, ours will be a life filled with love and laughter. What I'm asking is if you will do me the honor of becoming my wife?"

She nodded, but her voice wouldn't work. Tears were streaming down her face. He slid a ring onto her finger and got to his feet. There were tears on his cheeks. He looked down into her eyes.

"Yes," she finally managed to squeak.

He cupped his hands around the sides of her neck and looked down at her lips. Then he looked back into her eyes, and she nodded in the moment before he claimed her mouth in a kiss that told her so very eloquently just how much he loved her.

When they came up for air, everyone was clapping and congratulating them. Audrey hugged her, so did Ally and Brayden and Ted. All the friends that she'd already made here and the people she knew would become friends.

Little Sophie tugged on her hand. "Your ring is so pretty."

Izzy looked down at it. She'd been so caught up with Diego that she hadn't even noticed what the ring looked like. She was just thrilled that it was there.

Her mouth fell open when she saw it.

Maria appeared at her side. "Didn't he do well?"

Izzy spluttered. "It's … damn!"

Maria laughed. "That's what I thought, too. But then I should have known he has great taste. He chose you."

Izzy hugged her. "Thanks Maria."

"Thank you! I can't believe that I get such an awesome mother-in-law!"

Izzy smiled. "I never thought about that. I'll be your mother-in-law, won't I?"

Maria nodded happily. "And grandma to our babies."

Izzy's eyes filled with tears again.

Zack put his arm around her shoulders and pulled her into his side.

"Are you okay with this?" she asked him.

He leaned down and kissed her cheek. "I'm so much more than okay. And don't worry, I won't be a difficult stepson."

She laughed. "I'll try not to be a wicked stepmother. I've never been a mom before, though."

Zack tightened his arm around her shoulders, and she saw Diego come to stand beside Maria.

"I'm going to tell you something that even Maria doesn't know," said Zack.

Maria raised an eyebrow at him.

"You've made me almost as happy as you've made my dad, Izzy. Don't ever think that I'm not happy about this. You said you've never been a mom before; well, I've never *had* a mom before. I had a mother till I was six, but I don't really remember her. I used to wish that one day my dad would find a really awesome woman and get married." He grinned. "And today you made my wish come true."

Izzy swiped at her eyes. "Damn. You're going to have me bawling."

Diego wiped his sleeve across his face. "And me."

He came and put his arm around her. "Do you believe me now ... that we're family? That we want and need to be a family as much as you do?"

She nodded as she looked up into his eyes. "I believe you."

"Good."

Ted and Audrey came to stand with them. Audrey took hold of her hand to admire the ring. "It's beautiful, Iz."

Izzy looked at the diamond on her finger and then smiled at Diego. "It's big and in-your-face and gorgeous! What else should I have expected?"

Diego swaggered his shoulders. "Nothing less than the best for my beautiful wife."

Ted slapped his shoulder. "So, now we get to be each other's best man?"

Diego's smile faded, and he looked at Zack. Izzy understood straight away what he was thinking. He wouldn't want to have to choose between his son and his best friend.

She smiled and slipped her arm through Zack's. "Phew. And I thought you might ask my boy to be your best man."

Diego still looked uncertain.

"I'm kind of hoping that he'll walk me down the aisle."

Diego's eyes shone with tears again.

Zack smiled down at her happily. "It'd be my honor."

~ ~ ~

As they lay in bed that night, Diego curled his arm around her and hugged her to his chest. "I love you, Izzy."

"I love you more, Diego."

He chuckled. "Impossible."

She looked up into his eyes. "Don't you believe it. I love you to the ends of the earth and back again."

He smiled. "I love you all the way to where the rainbow ends."

She laughed. "Rainbows don't end."

"Exactly." He dropped a kiss on her lips. "My love for you will never end. You're going to be my wife, Izzy. I will love you until the day I die. And I promise I will do everything in my power to make you happy."

She smiled up at him. "I believe you. And I already know that you are a powerful man."

He winked at her. "But only when you want me to be."

"I do want you to be. I want you to be who you are."

It was true. He'd loved her past all her hang-ups, and she knew that he would love her until the day he died. This big, beautiful man had taught her what love and family really meant, and she intended to spend the rest of her days loving him and their family right back;

;

# A Note from SJ

I hope you enjoyed Diego and Izzy's story. Please let your friends know about the books if you feel they would enjoy them as well. It would be wonderful if you would leave me a review, I'd very much appreciate it.

Check out the "Also By" page to see if any of my other series appeal to you – I have a couple of ebook freebie series starters, too, so you can take them for a test drive.

There are a few options to keep up with me and my imaginary friends:

The best way is to Sign up for my Newsletter at my website www.SJMcCoy.com. Don't worry I won't bombard you! I'll let you know about upcoming releases, share a sneak peek or two and keep you in the loop for a couple of fun giveaways I have coming up :0)

You can join my readers group to chat about the books or like my Facebook Page  www.facebook.com/authorsjmccoy
I occasionally attempt to say something in 140 characters or less(!) on Twitter

And I'm in the process of building a shiny new website at www.SJMcCoy.com

I love to hear from readers, so feel free to email me at SJ@SJMcCoy.com if you'd like. I'm better at that! :0)

I hope our paths will cross again soon. Until then, take care, and thanks for your support—you are the reason I write!

Love

SJ

# PS Project Semicolon

You may have noticed that the final sentence of the story closed with a semi-colon. It isn't a typo. Project Semi Colon is a non-profit movement dedicated to presenting hope and love to those who are struggling with depression, suicide, addiction and self-injury. Project Semicolon exists to encourage, love and inspire. It's a movement I support with all my heart.

*"A semicolon represents a sentence the author could have ended, but chose not to. The sentence is your life and the author is you."* - Project Semicolon

This author started writing after her son was killed in a car crash. At the time I wanted my own story to be over, instead I chose to honour a promise to my son to write my 'silly stories' someday. I chose to escape into my fictional world. I know for many who struggle with depression, suicide can appear to be the only escape. The semicolon has become a symbol of support, and hopefully a reminder – Your story isn't over yet

# Also by SJ McCoy

**Summer Lake Silver**
Clay and Marianne in Like Some Old Country Song
Seymour and Chris in A Dream Too Far
Ted and Audrey in A Little Rain Must Fall
Izzy and Diego in Where the Rainbow Ends

**Summer Lake Seasons**
Angel and Luke in Take These Broken Wings
Zack and Maria in Too Much Love to Hide
Logan and Roxy in Sunshine Over Snow
Ivan and Abbie in Chase the Blues Away
Colt and Cassie in Forever Takes a While

**Summer Lake Series**
Love Like You've Never Been Hurt (FREE in ebook form)
Work Like You Don't Need the Money
Dance Like Nobody's Watching
Fly Like You've Never Been Grounded
Laugh Like You've Never Cried
Sing Like Nobody's Listening
Smile Like You Mean It
The Wedding Dance
Chasing Tomorrow
Dream Like Nothing's Impossible
Ride Like You've Never Fallen
Live Like There's No Tomorrow
The Wedding Flight

**Remington Ranch Series**
Mason (FREE in ebook form) and also available as Audio
Shane
Carter
Beau
Four Weddings and a Vendetta

**A Chance and a Hope**
Chance is a guy with a whole lot of story to tell. He's part of the fabric of both Summer Lake and Remington Ranch. He needed three whole books to tell his own story.

Chance Encounter
Finding Hope
Give Hope a Chance

**Love in Nashville**
Autumn and Matt in Bring on the Night

**The Davenports**
Oscar
TJ
Reid

**The Hamiltons**
Cameron and Piper in Red wine and Roses
Chelsea and Grant in Champagne and Daisies
Mary Ellen and Antonio in Marsala and Magnolias
Marcos and Molly in Prosecco and Peonies
**Coming Next**
Grady

# About the Author

I'm SJ, a coffee addict, lover of chocolate and drinker of good red wines. I'm a lost soul and a hopeless romantic. Reading and writing are necessary parts of who I am. Though perhaps not as necessary as coffee! I can drink coffee without writing, but I can't write without coffee.

I grew up loving romance novels, my first boyfriends were book boyfriends, but life intervened, as it tends to do, and I wandered down the paths of non-fiction for many years. My life changed completely a few years ago and I returned to Romance to find my escape.

I write 'Sweet n Steamy' stories because to me there is enough angst and darkness in real life. My favorite romances are happy escapes with a focus on fun, friendships and happily-ever-afters, just like the ones I write.

These days I live in beautiful Montana, the last best place. If I'm not reading or writing, you'll find me just down the road in the park - Yellowstone. I have deer, eagles and the occasional bear for company, and I like it that way :0)

CPSIA information can be obtained
at www.ICGtesting.com
Printed in the USA
LVHW021526210920
666682LV00002B/280